ADVENTURES OF BASTARD AND M.E.

ADVENTURES OF BASTARD AND M.E.

STEFAN O. RAK

For Michael,
Thank you
for doing what
you do.
with love and
respect,

Whisk(e)y Tit
NYC & VT

4.21.18

Published in the United States by Whisk(e)y Tit: www.whiskeytit.com. If you wish to use or reproduce all or part of this book for any means, please let the author and publisher know. You're pretty much required to, legally.

ISBN 978-0996764650

Library of Congress Control Number: 2018933264

Cover design by Ariadne Wetzler.

First Whisk(e)y Tit paperback edition.

CONTENTS

CENTERDAY (ONE)

POST-CENTERDAY (TWO)

MOONDAY (SIX)

WONDERDAY (SEVEN)

PRE-CENTERDAY (EIGHT)

CENTERDAY (NINE)

POST-CENTERDAY (TEN)

XERXES (ELEVEN)

CENTERDAY (ONE)

RENT YOUR BRAIN.

It was late morning when the phone call rang. Just before the Marker reached the Half-Day Signifier on the Circhronometer.

It was unusual for Bastard (not the Bastard) to be awake so early. He suffered from a chronic condition (one of many) that typically disabled him from waking up before the Time of One Major Mark after the aforementioned Half-Day Signifier signified its signification.

So far, the day had flowered as any other dayflower flowers, at least in relation to the flowers that had dayed since Bastard's reincarnation. For the proceeding daze of adventure are of Bastard's second life (note not necessarily significant, except that, in his previous life, Bastard had never paid attention to dayflowers – nor their flowering).

He stared at the tidy surface of his desk, which was never cluttered with papers – nor with anything else, for that matter – , because he had not much, and even less papers. As a recently professionalized private detective, he'd yet to land any work.

Maybe I should hire a new office? he said to himself as he engaged the desk in a routine game of mindless eye-casting. Then he sat up, and sipped at a cup that contained within an ever-depleting amount of absinthe-warmed-down equal parts liquid stimulant. It was whilst in the midst of this meditative idleness that the phone's ring rang.

No one had ever called him before.

Bastard sent his eyes around the room, scanning it for any clues as to where this noise was coming from and what meaning it bore. After a timed series of rings, a harsh BEEP sent his body to the floor. Hands over his ears, he was still able to hear a strange voice pronounce, seemingly unprompted, that Bastard was presently unavailable.

But it was obvious that Bastard was present – and available, because he had nothing to do.

While the un-attributable invisible mouth continued, unheeded, Bastard got up off the floor and strolled over to the kitchen. He opened the cooler, pulled out a sandwich, and watched the door close on its own. Amazing, he thought to himself. Then he began to unwrap the glass sheet he had utilized to preserve the prepared consummation's freshness, having made the delectable gustatory item earlier that year. Thin but durable whole wheat paper bread comprised seven-year-old foot-stomped mashed gooseberries, pigeon wing twig bones, flounder-bile marinated cat tail, thinly sliced *as well as* pressed dinosaur shallots, a thick slice of yeti lard topped with purple orange peels within a papier-mâché crust, all drowned in a madras corduroy lysergic acid dressing.

He stumbled into the bathroom, where he tossed the

glass wrapper into a garbage bag that was full of garbage that he would never throw away, took two bites of the sandwich and flushed it down the toilet. He pooped in the sink while brushing his teeth in the bath, dried himself off with a few half-threes of shoes, and, resuming his seat at his desk, adopted a sense of sophistication in order to press some blinking button light on a black box on his desk, which said,

"Bastard. It's M.E.. Meet at our old spot. Soon as you can."

He recognized the voice immediately, even though it was one he had not heard in many, many Circles.

The Circhronometer on the wall looked at him and said, "Eleven forty fifty p h d."

"Give me fifteen, I'll be there prior," Bastard noised into the black box but at the Circle-Keeper.

As Bastard gathered his things in preparation to leave his office, I decided to accompany him. Then, I did.

It was a sunny day in the city of Metropolisse, and very cloudy.

Bastard exited the building and crossed the street, his eyes lowering from the sky below to the street above, between which he tasted a billboard advertisement splattered upon one of the new condominiums (one of many that were ejaculating all over the city at that Time).

"RENT YOUR BRAIN," it shouted in big black letters on a yellow back. In quieter print below, "One thousand balls per week. Painless and risk-free. Call now!" Below that, telephonic contact data. And most hush-hush, "We promise not to sell any private or personal information to any alien entities without first drawing your blood."

The sign was signed by Free-Enterprise 999.

Bastard didn't break step, just kept walking.

THE HEADS OF THE ORGANIZATION REUNITE.

Miguel Evangelista was sitting at a table in the corner by the window. As Bastard approached his old friend, he calculated about three decimals since their last encounter. They shook hands formally, like best friends do.

"So," Bastard cringed in pain as he sat down, smiling, "what are you doing back in Nation? Correct me if I'm wrong, but your Physical Presence Privilege was revoked some Time ago. Eternal External Exile. Never to be allowed back within the border that protects our great Kingdom from the lesser and most disgusting lands beyond. Right?"

"You're not wrong," his friend answered. "In fact, in that sense, you are right. However, I've been granted temporary amnesty for one week. They've flown M.E. here to testify at Grand Justice Court."

"Hm. And the Magistrates let you back in for that?"

"Appears so, man. I volunteered, and they offered.

Seems they're desperate. They really wanna get this guy – public enemy number ten, and for some Time. And only I know who he is." M.E. inhaled and then exhaled.

Bastard regarded his friend. The face had aged a bit, but he knew that this was M.E..

"Listen. I don't have much Time. We need to start working now. Today is Centerday. The Official Conditional Beneficial Absolute Judicial Hearing is to be held on Wonderday. Next day, I'm out. Back down Beyond South. And them ain't fucking around. If I don't catch that flying saucer on Time, ...well, they promised – in writing – that they will torture M.E. through life to death. Maybe even through death to life again. Bring M.E. back like they did you," his wide dark eyebrows arched and his eyes danced around a fire, naked.

Someone in a shaved head and brown kimono interrupted them with a harmless whisper. "Would you mind something to drink?"

Bastard pointed at Miguel's glass, trying not to appear too anxious. The stranger turned around and left.

M.E. pushed his glass towards Bastard, who smiled, dehydrated. He took a decent hit and slid it back. Some Time passed. Others stayed.

"All right," Miguel began. But then M.E. had to pause at the return of the attender, who set down a glass with Bastard's whiskey. He tasted it good.

Bastard and M.E. hadn't seen each other since B ran that stretch, and that was years before he first died. The conversation meandered through the evening. Getting high and getting drunk, they caught up and talked a lot of shit. Love was clear.

"All right," Bastard resumed. "You gotta tell me: who are you testifying against? What's the case?"

"Ah yes! You'll like this: me."[1]

"What?"

"You heard M.E.."

"All right. Go on."

"Remember the Guns and Butter Scandal of 293?"

"How could I forget? It was all over the announcements some Time ago." Bastard paused. He looked at M.E., who leaned in a fraction of a degree to confirm his singular role orchestrating that scandal. Bastard grinned and exclaimed, "Ha!"

"That's right! They have no idea, of course. They're looking for a highly developed being named Newt 'Newt' Humbert. Clever little fellow. And I have hard evidence against the man – enough to put him away for all rotations to come. So they're bringing M.E. in as an I Witnessed."

Bastard's grin widened beyond what seemed physically possible, or at the very least proportional and comfortable. "And you're not afrayed they might catch ontwo you?"

"First of all, no," M.E. nearly offended! "Second of all, no. Thirdly, the information that I have for the Court will lead them to conclude, beyond a Shadow of a Doubt, the absolute and unquestionable guilt of one Mr. Newt Humbert – while at the same Time leading them further and further down the wrong track course that they'd have to pedal seventy-twice at point four three seconds per horn rim on a tiny tandem bicycle before they could catch up with M.E.." Bastard's friend snickersed. "Fourthermore, if you remember, I wasn't here when that shit went down. I'd already been Exiled…" M.E. looked around the room.

"So…okay. Aight. Quick though – for the record –

---

1. M.E. can say the word "me" in this context because he's not talking about M.E. (he's talking about Newt Humbert).

Newt Humbert's a dude, right? Not a slimy little amphibious creature?"

"Yes and no. He is a person-man. He's not little, but he is slimy and slightly amphibious. It's his real name though, for real. I mean, I gave it to him. He's my creation. So he doesn't exist outside of my mind, then theirs, and now yours."

"So why do they call him 'Newt?'"

"What? That's his first name. Just call him Newt. You don't have to say 'Newt.'"

The bald kimono arrived with more liquor juice. When s/he left them, Bastard considered aloud, "So, officially, you are here for this official reason, which is not an officious reason for your being here, nor for my being to hear. I don't think I get it, my dear friend. You have nothing to benefit from testifying in the Guns and Butter Trial. And as much as I know that you love me, I'm ware awell that I'm not the soul purpose for your detourn to the Nation.

"So...am I within reason to conclude that you intend to benefit from this visit otherways?" Bastard pawed his whiskey glass, spinning it in its approximate place. With his eyes, he looked at M.E.'s eyes. "What are you doing here, for real for real?"

"Well, Bastard: we have work to do. I need your help organizing the Organization's new operation for organized confusion. Needed to see you in person, and wanted to be here for the initial stages. I need your help putting together a crew."

"What do we need?"

"We need an operator, a safecracker, a master planner, probably one or two form-fitters, a munitions specialist, a cat burglar... Other needs will present themselves. I have Haile Leburik and Doctor Diemande already on board."

"Consider it done. What're we talking about?"

"Free-Enterprise 999. You passed a billboard on your way here."

"As you know."

I nodded, but said nothing.

"F-E 999 is our key to the lock on the door that opens to a room full of balls. I need you to look into F-E 999, find out everything you can. Who they are, where they are, what game they're playing, how they keep score. All that shit."

"What's our endgame?"

"Can't share that yet. Of course, I can, but I don't want to, I guess, probably because it isn't important at the moment. I'm waiting for some news from the South; then, we're on. Your immediate mission: find us a way into F-E 999's main control room. We need to get in there to fuck with their pooters. I don't know how we'll manage this, but I have no doubt in your abilities. You will always be the most charming con I know, Bastard; I am certain of this and little else."

"Thank you for your appreciation," he replied. "What do we have on them already?"

"Quite a lot, my lighter-skinned brother. But I have even more than that." Bastard waited for M.E. to continue. "I'm confident that I know what they're up to...and if I'm right, then we are in a position to make enormous balls. It'll be our biggest job to date. Serious risks. Elephantine returns." M.E. smiled. "And judging from your current listing in the Cellephonic Peoples-Locator Handbook, you could use the balls." Pause. "What's the fuck is you doing as a private dick, anyway?"

"Why? You think I should go public?"

"Ha," they giggled.

"But for real, to answer your question: nothing,"

Bastard proudly desponded. "I've had this business card for several hands now – haven't had the opportunity to play it. No work yet."

"That's wonderful!" M.E. congratulated his friend.

"Yes, it's been great," Bastard smiled. "Back to the footwork in hand. I'll get on top and underneath this F-E 999 shit, and I'll put together a crew. You said the trial come Wonderday?"

"Yeh man. Gives us five switches to launch this shit. Not nearly enough Time, meaning way too much. Meantime, I have to go about the preliminary procedures for the trial. I've several meetings with my lawyers, my lawyers' lawyers, the prosecutor's lawyers, their lawyers' lawyers, their lawyers' mothers, their mothers' daughters, the lawyers' daughters (that's personal, actually, not business); and the legal representatives of Guns, as well as of Butter, plus the newly formed Coalition for the Protection of Civic Oppression by the Citizens' Interests Representing the Production, Preservation, Propaganda, Distribution, Anti-Abolition, and Fair Trade of Dairy Products and Firearms. And of course Newt Humbert's lawyers, who have no apparent scruples defending someone they've never met and never will, who's definitely guilty, and who won't be at the trial, because he doesn't fucking exist." The two friends shared a double smile, on a cone, with rainbow sprinkles. "Leave now, and return even sooner with your findings and our crew."

Bastard downed the rest of his grain and stood up, reaching into his pants. "Put your balls away, it's on M.E.." They shook hands. "F-E 999. Get into it, deep. This part is all you. We need to get in there. I'll see you tomorrow at thirty seven, okay?"

"Okay."

"Okay."

"Okay."

3

SOMETIMES A WOMAN'S VOICE ALONE.

On his way back to the office from the bar, Bastard wrote down the phone number from the F-E 999 advertisement...the phone number, and he dialed it as soon as he had reassumed his seat in his chair after entering the building, ascending the escalator wing-shaft to the thirty-third floor, passing down the hallway to his door, click clack brown shoes sole linoleum floor, unlocking his front door, and walking to behind his desk.

"Thank you for calling Free-Enterprise 999. If you know your party's extension, why did you call this number? If you are calling to claim your free chance to win a lifetime prescription to your choice of pd=t disc replacements, please press one. If you are calling regarding our extremely popular Rent Your Brain program, press two. If you are calling to place an order with our equally popular Licensed Pharmaceutical Distribution Center, press three. If you are calling to register a compliment, press four. Employment opportunities, five. If you are calling regarding any legal issues, please hang the fuck up now. To hear your options again, please hang up first, then press the Redial button on your telephone touchpad, and you may experience déja-vû. Fuck, this is exhausting."

Bastard hung up the phone and thought about his options. He rolled a cigarette, smoked it, took a nip from his flask. After considering the choices and calculating what was hopefully the best approach, he decided to call again from a pay phone out on the street outside.

Where he dialed the number again. This Time, however, he heard something else. "If you are calling regarding Rent Your Brain, this offer is temporarily unavailable. Everything else is the same."

"Fuck," Bastard. He decided to press the third button.

A woman's voice said, "Free-Enterprise 999, Licensed Pharmaceutical Distribution Center. My name is Des, how may I assist you."

"I'd like to place an order for a gross dilaudid. They still make that, right?"

"No problem. Just one gross?"

"Nah, make it gross gross."

"That's a lot."

"Hehehe. Yeh."

"Whatever. Your address, please?"

Bastard gave her his P.O.'s Box.

"Okay. Your Voicebank has been deducted the sum of forty-nine and seven balls. You will also receive, ninety percent complimentary, a ninety second meatball rebate with your purchase, valid at participating Interplanetary Scuba Diving Inc. Underwater Restaurants, Hotels, Spas, Baths, Torture Chambers, and Pits of Doom Nation-Narrow. Thank you for calling F-E 999 and have a happy day."

"Wait a second – Dess?"

"No, it's Des."

"Okay, got it, sorry. My name is Bastard," said Bastard. "Do you like your job?"

"I'm afraid I'm not qualified to answerve that question. Happy day."

"Qualified? I don't think that's the right word. Anyway, hold up. I'm sorry. I'm looking for work, that's all."

"I'm afraid we're not hiring, Bastard, but if you'd like, you may leave a message with our employment center."

"Thanks but no thanks. I want to talk to you." He decided to take a chance. "I'd like to see you."

Silence.

More silence.

Longer.

Then more.

Then, "Meet me at the BrainLiver Cafe tomorrow fifteen. That's when and where I take my afternoon stimulants."

He was surprised that she agreed, and hung up the phone without saying, "Goodbye."

Once back in his office, he fixed up, and slowly sipped several scotches until he passed out for a bit.

4

ASSEMBLAGE.

Bastard spent the rest of the day making contact with some old friends.

M.E. had said that they needed "an operator, a safecracker, a master planner, probably one or two form-fitters, a weapons specialist, a cat burglar... Other needs will present themselves. I have Haile Leburik and Doctor Diemande already on board." Yes; that is what M.E. said.

Bastard knew Leburik and Diemande well, and he was looking forward to seeing them again. The fact that these two science experts were involved suggested to Bastard that the operation had something to do with having to know science. This much, he was certain, he knew.

Since the purpose of the mission was to do something technical inside Free-Enterprise 999's main control room, he started with the role of Operator.

The Mechanic was Bastard's first pick. The man was not, as his name suggests, a contract killer. Rather, he lived his name by illegally fixing People's computer machines, as well as other technological, mechanical, and analog things with problems. His real name was Macchine, which is pretty funny. However, he thought that name was too obvious, so he literally changed the letteral order.

The Mechanic had a record; but when he was caught and tried, he didn't have a turntable, so the Magistrates gave him eighteen. Hoping that this term had ended and the man was around, Bastard set out in search of the Organization's best Operator.

Without much effort, Bastard found the Mechanic lounging about the old factory yards by the Dirty Water River. They used to go there together to watch the abandoned buildings burn and smoke and crumble, so it was the first place he looked.

The fires were still burning, the smoke still smoldering, the walls still falling away. It would never end; Bastard knew this as an absolute.

The two characters were very pleased to see each other. Without going into much detail, the Mechanic readily agreed to join up.

"Damn, dude. Miguel Evangelista and Bastard. Two motherfuckers I thought I'd never see again."

"Why is that, man?"

"Huh? Because M.E. was banished and you died."

"Oh, right."

They laughed at Bastard's space cadet-edness, "Ha ha ha," in unison.

Then, "Aight man. Let's roll."

The Mechanic popped himself off the concrete steps upon which he had been sitting. Whatever those stairs had led to was long gone; Bastard appreciated this.

Side by side, they walked away from the black river, back to the hood.

From the Mechanic, Bastard learned who was dead now, who was still around and working. And with his help, Bastard would succeed in assembling an ideal team.

They located the highly skilled form-fitters Sasia Stasia and NNannette Nonet with ease. The two criminalesses were hanging out on the corner of their block. It was their corner; in fact, it's where Bastard had seen them last, before his death.

Although Sasia and NNannette weren't conjoined twins nor related to each other by blood, they often spoke the same words at the same Times. Not always, thankfully, because that could be annoying. Each was an individual; they were very close, but not the same.

"What, have you two moved at all since I seen you?"

Shock and confusion and excitement as they clocked Bastard's image, and then exclaimed, "Oh shit!!! Look who's back, black!" Smiles on all faces. "What's happenin', baby?" The old friends embraced lovingly.

"Glad you asked," Bastard chuckled. "Check this: M.E. is in town."

"Fuck off."

"Yup. Long story. But I'll let M.E. tell you, because he is a better story-teller. We're putting something together. You wanna work? You'll have to leave the corner, though."

"You're still an ass! It's nice to see that you are true, as always. And yeah! For sure. We're down."

A hot wind blew from off the river and down the streets, and although it smelled bad, Bastard inhaled deeply. He was good.

POST-CENTERDAY
(TWO)

5

THE "F" AND THE "E" DO NOT STAND FOR "FUCK EVERYONE."

The BrainLiver Cafe was an obnoxious place for tight-assed businesspersons and rehabilitated convicted anti-Conspirator leprechauns. Bastard was there to meet with Des, the lady from the F-E 999 telephone.

He didn't have to wait for her long enough to say that he really actually waited. For, presently, Des appeared in a calm flurry – as if the wind had escorted her, carried her and deposited her in the chair at the table across from Bastard.

"Did you want dilaudid or a job?" she aimed and fired.

"Both."

"Don't bullshit me," she proclaimed sadly. "I have half a Circle for Me Break Time. What do you want? Why did you want to see me? And more importantly, how did you know that I wanted to see you?" She glanced around the room nervously and unbelievably. "And how did I know that I wanted to see you?" Bastard thought that last question was unnecessary and silly, but he didn't say so out loud. "That was some risk you took. You're lucky it wasn't fatal."

"We always know," Bastard bullshat like a true Jokerman Infidel. "But that's not important." Precisely upon completing that last sentence, he resumed. "Do you like your job, Des?"

I staid silent.

"I asked you not to waste my measure, my valuable waist, my Me Time." She inhaled a heavy load and looked down at her dew-baked sunflower leopard tail muffin tops. Then back at Bastard's two eyes she sighed, "Do you want to start over, or should I walk out now?"

"All right, lady. Easy. I'll connect the lines for as straight a dot as possible to you, for you, so that we may reach it sooner, together. To answer your question, I want to know about this Rent Your Brain business. What do you know?"

"It expired for -"

"Now you're bullshitting me," he cut her off.

Des started bleeding. "You needn't have done that," blushing.

"Maybe I did," he exalted.

She smirked, and Bastard began to cry. Des donated him her napkin, and they fell in love.

"And who are you, again?" she asked. "Which one are you? Why am I here, why am I talking with you? Why am I?"

"You know, I could never figure out the answer to that last one. Can't say. I'd like to know why I am I."

"You're a smart-ass."

"And now you're playing me," Bastard reshuffling his feet. He awkwardly shifted his focus from one hand to the other, as he was supporting the weight of his body with an arm-tightening cum hand-pressing (down on the seat) up in an effort to ease his back pain. "You charged my voice, and I told you my name. You know who I am – and you know full well what I'm full of."

"Yeah. Shit."

Bastard went to poop. When he returned, "The reason I wanted to talk to you, after all these moonages, is to make you an offer. (Oh, and speaking of offers, I don't want that lifetime pd=t disc replacement shit. I know pain, and I know about pd=t discs. Just because it's different doesn't mean it's better.)"

Unparenthetically he continued, "It's pretty straight: we need information. You have access to this information – so we need your help. And if you help us, we will be very grateful." He wasn't sure if that was enticing enough.

Des didn't speak. Bastard looked in her green gray brown hazel eyes and formed an even smile. The woman before him was absolutely fucking gorgeous.

He watched her as she touched her silver gray hair and kind of moved it, brushing a few soft stalks away from her eyes. He did not yet know that her silver gray hair was blond at night. Some of the strays graced her pitted dark olive skin face, while some rested; others caressed her neatly formed shoulders with the suppleness that only hairfingers can touch. An angular, but not offensively so, nose accentuated her uprisen cheek bones and carefully landscaped eye-brows and -lashes. She wore a body that would make any man's head turn twice. Bastard broke some ten necks before he accepted that this was a natural reaction.

She had yet to answer. He wasn't sure if she was expecting him to continue. He began to question whether or not he had said anything. Then he bolstered, "Furthermore, I promise you enormous balls if you cooperate. And if we succeed, you will be rewarded beyond your wildest dreams – unless your dreams are really, really wild. But maybe even still."

He pulled out and lit a cigarette in an attempt to distract himself. He wasn't sure what she was playing at – if she was playing at all, which he was pretty sure she was. "And I will personally welcome you into – "

The sandwiches arrived, though no one had ordered them. The server set the parts on the table, and Bastard and Des began to put them together. They laughed during this assemblage, parlaying stories about childhood occurrences, which Bastard had to invent since he had never been a child. They fell in love with each other again.

He placed a sliver of a ridged pickle slice on her tongue, which naturally existed inside her mouth, beyond her lips, in a moist cavity in her face.

I looked at mine, but it remained on the plate, silent.

When Des finished eating, Bastard properly wiped his mouth with a napkin. Then she said, "Okay."

"Word? Fucking great. First, I'm curious. Is your name short for something? Sorry I misspelled the pronunciation earlier." It's not that Bastard couldn't spell; he'd just forgotten her name. "Is it – "

"Des. Despi. Short for Despi'kha. Last name Belle. Only my closest loved ones call me Despi'kha Belle. Others call me Despi. To even others, it's Des."

"That's a beautiful sequence."

"Stop. Go. I said I'm down."

"Okay." So, "What the fuck is Free-Enterprise 999? Who's behind it? And why do they hyphenate 'Free' and 'Enterprise?' It makes no sense. And what are they doing with the brains that they rent?"

"How do I know I can trust you?"

"I guess you can't. Hmm," Bastard tried to think of

something and failed. "Tell me again – what's your name?"

"Des. I just fucking told you."

"Right. Bastard," he volunteered.

"I know." She drank from her glass. Bastard joined her, drinking from her glass.

"I hope I'm doing the right thing..." she shuddered, but not necessarily reflexively. "First of all, Free-Enterprise 999 has no business with that hyphen."

"And the – ?"

"The Rent Your Brain business? It's mental slavery capitalism," she dropped. "The company tempts the People with balls. And the People come, because the People always want balls. They voluntarily give up their brains for one week. During that week, the patients/patrons are neutralized, and F-E 999 has unlimited access to their brains."

Bastard didn't say anything.

"Our doctors surgically implant various neo-neurological receptors of our own design. These artificial receptors communicate with the brain, they communicate whatever we've programmed." She quickly fingered her ear canal. "The invasive surgical procedure takes about a week, after which we release the suckers with their balls.

"Then, from F-E 999's Neuro Transmission Center, we begin the individualized and invisible broadcasts of specific sonic stimuli simuli, which tackle and tickle the implanted receptors."

Des paused for effect. It was good, because it made her next sentence sound more important.

"Do you get it, yet? F-E 999 is able to impose physiological and psychological dependency – without the introduction of any physical chemical. Addiction enslavement for mind control for profit. When we cease transmitting to them, they begin to suffer a debilitating withdrawal. Seemingly inexplicably. They need help, and they come to us. They know that F-E 999 will provide them with free medical care and free script-writing. Of course, the newly addicted pay for the drugs, which they purchase exclusively from our Licensed Pharmaceutical Distribution Center. We recoup that thousand balls within days.

"It's supply and demand, and we set the demand for our supply. We know what they need, and we have what they need. We own them. Guaranteed, lifetime, custom-made consumers. We control their brains." She took a deep breath, for she had used a lot of words. "It's really pretty brilliant."

"I agree," because he did.

"Got it?" she inquired finally but softly.

"I think so, maybe; for sure though," Bastard wondered. His mind thoughts rapidly proceeded through all probable scenarios of possible realities that might result from F-E 999's machinations. He processed imagined intentions and effectualizations and meanings. "I must admit, it's very clever. Who's behind it?"

6

BASTARD COMES INSIDE THE PLASTIC BAG.

His question inspired anxiety within her. She insisted that they leave, immediately, separately – and that Bastard meet her, presently, at another place.

Apparently, Me Break Time doesn't mean to her what it means to other People, I remember Bastard thinking. The notion troubled him, but not as much as it turned him on.

She collected her random loose shit (like her metallic handkerchief and soft pen) while getting up from the table. So seemingly easily, so fluidly, she had combined two different acts into one seamless move.

Bastard was impressed, deeply affected. *This woman has conquered Mathematics!*

His brain sent some information to his heart.

His heart answered, *That's not my job.*

She had lovely legs. He watched them legs carry her body out the door. He gathered that they had to meet elsewhere, but he did not know why – the two of them, not her legs. Then he thought about where her legs met.

After a medium-rare circle, per Despi's instructions, Bastard pushed himself away and up from the table. He exited the inner-organic BrainLiver Cafe. Following in her footsteps, he crossed the street and entered the Plastic Bag.

Treading carefully, he found Des with little difficulty. He assessed the seating arrangement and doubted that he could fit at the table. Somehow it worked out okay.

Sitting, Bastard surveyed the new location.

The Plastic Bag was in a small space. It had plastic tables and chairs. Everything was white and bright. Bastard felt a headache approaching.

He regarded the little workers, who were of normal size when Bastard wasn't dusted. But since inhaling some burning Phencyclidine on his short walk across the street, everything appeared disproportionate.

Another everything was served in plastic bags. That was the gimmick. Food, beverages, ether, amyl nitrate, melted air and even frozen cheese. All in plastic bags, priced depending on weight or dose. Patrons were encouraged to return their empty plastic bags, which were repurposed as feed for machinic-aquatic life.

Des seemed annoyed by having to wait for Bastard to give her his attention. Then, she continued their conversation by answering the question Bastard had posed at the BrainLiver Cafe.

"An elderly entrepreneur is behind all of this. Incubated Herbert Algernon. Goes by the name of Lance Newcomb. Has ties to an Ancient Family, or so some say. Certainly something dark about the man. He tries to cover it up by wearing pink chiffon shirts. Don't know which Ancient Family, unfortunately. Though many say, 'There is only one.'

"Rumor has it," she wouldn't stop talking yet, "he's the Grand Vampire. Who knows."

"Holy fucking shit," Bastard's mind was blown – away, not apart. "I know the name. Holy fuckshit. You're blowing my mind. Away, not apart."

"Yup. I see."

"What else can you tell me?"

"Well, Lance Newcomb spearheaded the no longer top-secret Crack Alchemy Project for the Magistrates. So theM owe him for that. Which is why they let him profit madly through his various criminal enterprises without consequence. They say he's an Untouchable."

"Ech," Bastard scoffed. "Not to M.E., Des. Not to the Organization." Bastard felt better about how this was going. He coughed, and looked at her eyeballs. "Tell me: why is the Rent Your Brain offer over?"

"Seriously?"

"I see," he hrumphed. "Are you willing to work with us?"

"You haven't told me what we're doing."

"Good."

7

WHERE DO THE CATS GO WHEN IT RAINS (IT IS NOT RAINING, BECAUSE THERE ARE NO CATS).

Bastard considered what to say next.

"Okay," he said to her and himself as he tried to piece together the story puzzle that M.E. had set out. Then he laughed because he thought it was funny that M.E. hadn't told him what the picture would end up looking like. Then he laughed again because he knew that M.E. knew that both of them would be amused. Once again, he felt grateful for his friend's friendship.

"Here's what I need from you. I mean – how close are you to the mainframe? Whatever the fuck it's called?"

"Physically? Or emotionally?"

"Yes."

"The Neuro Transmission Center, right? Just wanna make sure we're talking about the same thing."

"Yeah, sure – I mean to say: Yes, the Neuro-Transmission Center, thank you. Fuck is up with all these fucking hyphenates?"

"You don't need the hyphen there, it's just Neuro Transmission Center. And I can't answer for my emotional distance. Physically, though, I am near." Her eyelid-lashes fluttered like the way that other things that flutter flutter. "But I don't work very closely with it."

"Aight. That was not helpful. We need to get into the NTC. Tomorrow night. Don't ask me why. Not yet. Ask me tomorrow? I may know by then." Bastard was getting excited. "How many people work in the core of the Center within F-E 999?"

"The Corporation employs three citizens at the core. Four of them work directly with and within the main NTC. (There is only one, so that one is the main one.)"

"Do you know them?" Bastard prodded.

"Of course I know them. There are only three."

"And do they trust you?"

"More than I trust you!" she accidentally shouted.

He frowned. "Go on."

"More than they should, apparently," Des smiled a wicked one that Bastard liked.

"Nice recovery," he sighed.

She sensed his disappointment, and then realized something about herself. Her face tightened, then relaxed. A genuine warmth replaced her prior lukewarmth. Without having moved an inch, she was now much closer to him.

It was her eyes. And that gaze. But those eyes. Fresh sensitivity and newborn care.

"Look," she softly but confidently spoke. "Whatever the fuck you're asking me... – whatever the fuck you're doing... I'll do it. I want to do it." She scoped his face, scored him up and down, locked her hazel pearls, pulled him in.

For a very brief moment – a moment that grew

shorter with each passing smaller moment, Bastard felt unusually outra-conscious. It was good that he got over it quickly.

Cause she moved fast.

"Okay, Bastard. Listen. Hear me out. I have my reasons for talking to you. I know about you and M.E.. I know your history. Your record. Your affiliations, your associations. It's all public fucking record, so don't be that impressed.

"I know that you died," she went on. "And I know that your death was your own doing."

This made Bastard uncomfortable, humanizing him for a moment. "That's one theory," Bastard attempted.

"I find that interesting," she didn't even need to brush it off. "I am aware that you are the Minister of the Interior of the Organization, for the Organization. You preside over a vast army of sorts. And that nobody knows who you are. Not even M.E.."

Her knowledge of his lives impressed him.

She waited for Bastard to finish huffing some ether.

"What I don't know, however, is why you're trying to be a private detective. Or how you're alive again. How that's even possible. You died. And yet, you are here. And... – I don't know if I care to know. Maybe it's just one of the many, many somethings that I will never know. And that is fine."

"I like you a lot," Bastard interrupted. He didn't know what they were talking about anymore, and he wanted to stop. Trying to swallow some dry spit, he said, "For now, all I need to know is this: can you get us into the building – into Free-Enterprise 999? Will you help us break into the NTC?"

"I think so, B."

"Please, call me Bastard. Only my best friends call me 'B.'"

He was happy to set the record straight. However, someone else had just done so, and the song resumed. It was a new and very popular ditty, the usual assembly line shit, replete with cloying fake voices that clawed at non-existent notes with awkwardly thick titanium fingers. The tune's only redeeming qualities were its temporal brevity, ignorability, and forgettability.

Bastard found himself (which was good) entertaining ordinary romantic notions and duly chastised himself. He intended to shrug off his disingenuous self-disgust, but instead involuntarily shuttered a burp.

"Whatever, Bastard. I like you, too; but you are a bit odd."

"Doesn't matter."

"Okay."

"Will you kiss me now?"

"I would like that."

He permitted the impulsive act of his hand reaching under the table to find hers, accepting. She held his hand gently, then gripped his wrist tightly. He leaned forward to give her more. She performed a similar physical act, though she leaned in at her hips and extended her neck, whereas Bastard's bodily conduct relied more upon arching his back and pushing his upper body forward. Their lips met with a profound sublimity that spoke of consciously communicated ferocious desire.

And so they kissed, and it was nice.

8

DO NOT BE SURPRISED IF A WINGED THING FLIES;
AND DO NOT BE SURPRISED WHEN IT DOES NOT.
(ALSO INCLUDED: A DATE WITH CURIOSITY.)

After, Bastard continued to recruit for the taskforce, and succeeded in accomplishing nothing. At thirty seven, he arrived for the scheduled meet.

He didn't see M.E..

Bastard grabbed a stool, guided it closer, and took it. He changed his mind and gave it back. Instead, he decided to utilize it, and placed himself on it so as to better order a bottle of grain at the bar.

While he waited, I recalled how Bastard and M.E. had first met at the First International Summit for Illegal Drug Traffickers, which back then was held at an undisclosed locution in the Ninth Sector of the Third Hemisphere of the Nolands. Bastard had somehow received an invitation, and Curiosity persuaded him to attend. She was a fine woman – he never could turn Curiosity down.

At the conference's first night gala dinner, the odd couple happened to be tabled with M.E.. Bastard and Curiosity reproached their assigned plates, facing Miguel Evangelista, who sat in his chair like a king on a pretty shitty throne. M.E. was surrounded by an army of opaque androgynous nymphoids, two of which who, at the command of a palpable mental hairbrush stroke (punctuated with invisible dental air-rinse wipe), vanished as soon as Bastard and his date planted their asses on the chairs that they had fraction-moment-shy occupied.

The dining room of the main hall was larger than many decent-sized outhouses, but no bigger than seventy-five bowling alleys. A sole soul pianist played symphonic orchestral solo works on the ceiling in the furthest corner nearest them. The remaining opaque androgynous nymphoids at the table smiled at the newly arrived couple, though it was unclear just why, why they would be smiling, and whether their smiles were sincere...

Miguel Evangelista immediately struck the two of them, twelve hectares later, as charismatic as enigmatic. Luckily, it was with a rubber bat. The man appeared extraordinary, sporting a tailored black horsefly suit, a violet shirt of velvet, a black polar-bear-dermis tie, and matching praying mantis leather belt ant shoes and watch. M.E. sat at the table with an air of natural command – perfectly unassuming, but which ate quite thoroughly. When Bastard introduced himself, the two shook hands as if they had never met.

That evening, all of the guests feasted on exquisite lobster aureole ravioli, a most delicate shark foot bisque, and a minimally braised miniature mammoth steak served on a bed of linen greens, topped with a robust, dark cherry feral feline blood reduction.

That was the night's menu, and those are the things that they ate. The conversations they had during this fateful meal, the laughs they shared, the discovery of mutual values, the love of truth and hatred of hypocrisy that was the fundamental foundation of each man's lives, marked the beginning of the lifelong and profitable friendship between Bastard and M.E..

That was a long time ago.

As Bastard approached his second bottle, a robotman approached him and repeated, "Your party is waiting."

Standing up, he thought about manythings, and as he walked towards M.E., he further pondered some of them.

Eight or nine opaque white androgyns sat surrounding M.E. around the round table. Bastard turned the neck of his head. He never liked the opaque androgyns.

When he looked back, M.E. sat alone. "Sorry about the freaks," said M.E.. "I forgot how you get. They're good minions. You should get used to them."

Bastard laughed, then said something that I didn't catch.

M.E. smiled, "I am glad." A delicate grimace was a prelude to a soulful smirk. "Yeh... Yeh. Brother, I am sorry that what went down went down the way that it went down."

"Why you bringing up old shit? We have new shit to eat on this table. And anyway...aaeeeeccchhh, don't be," Bastard dismissed. "It was how it went." He pulled in some air and put on his level smile before cracking up and exclaiming, "Man! When wind came in that you had exited the Greater Nation's Greater Water

Territories...that you had actually really made it...all the way out...that you were free... Damn, brother. I was very happy that day."

The two spoke at Length but to each other. It was safe for Bastard and M.E. to talk at Length because he was deaf. And although he was a fluent lip reader of twenty-nine languages that arguably don't exist, Length was also blind. Even if he was able to hear and see, he would never say anything to anyone, partly because he was mute. And beyond all of that, if he had all of his faculties and senses, it still would have been safe for Bastard and M.E. to talk, because he was an old friend. Length was a lifetime ghoster of farms. He wasn't a fucking rat.

For real for real, Bastard wasn't sure why Length was there. In fact, he wasn't even sure that his name was Length, or why he thought he knew the guy's name. The man had somehow appeared at their table, and was there now. Since they'd known him forever, Bastard and M.E. were not concerned. And until he left, they spoke as if he wasn't even there.

"We are what we are and we do what we do. Like guns. We know what we do is what we do, and we know we may have to do other things because of what we do. We know the risks. Better me than you, right?"

"This calls for a bottle." Miguel Evangelista summoned the server and ordered a bottle of the finest grain. "Of like you are a rarity," complimenting Bastard. "You understand that most of these objects aren't real," his arm fanning in extension beyond the here space to encompass all of the stationary and moving things that were.

Two glasses and one bottle on the table; the server left with the ice bucket and M.E.'s disapproving eyes at his back. Bastard filled the glasses and capped the bottle.

"Crew? Where we at."

"We good."

"Word!" Evangelista upped his eyeglasses. "Aight aight, that is very exciting! And what did you get on F-E 999, Rent Your Brain?"

They bumped glasses and took a hit.

Bastard's thoughts detoured in appreciation of the flavor carpet. He carefully swashed the liquid around his mouth like an exquisitely trained automatic clothing washer on the gentlest of cycles. The sweet fire of the hooch covered his tongue and sank into the sides inside and all the way to the back end of his flapper's cavern.

Unfortunately, I cannot describe how it tasted because it is like nothing that you know, and I didn't get to taste it.

"First and foremost, I ordered a gross gross of hydromorphone. I'll let you know when I get it." M.E. looked pleased. "Second, I made an ally today. From the place," pointing not in the proper direction. "Her name is Des. Despi. Not Despina, though: Despi'kha. Weird. She's agreed to help us."

Bastard then shared with M.E. what he had learned about F-E 999 and the Rent Your Brain business.

"The woman told me that F-E 999 rents brains for a week. They install these neo-neurological receptors, which enable them to stimulate the parts of the brain that respond to whatever drugs their pharmaceutical division is selling. They pay the suckers off with a thousand balls – who then proceed to purchase over a million balls of pharmaceuticals per annum.

"Now that F-E 999 has this access to their brains, they send out waves that target specific receptors. As we both know, different drugs work on different areas of the brain. And F-E 999 sells a variety of drugs. Their main business is in narcotic analgesics and farm wax, for the obvious reason of severity of addiction. So they usually start with the opiates: they trigger those receptors and the subject gets high. By the end of a couple weeks, they're hooked. And F-E 999 ceases transmission. In order to function, they gotta go buy the drugs – and of course, they get 'em from F-E 999..." When he finished, he breathed.

Across the table, his friend took a long, slow draw from his drink, as if hoping the act would lead to enlightenment. Then, M.E. drew his head back on a piece of paper, in pencil, and admitted, "I have to confess, B: I knew all of this before I charged you. Your initial task was the most effective way to brief you, to inform you of what's happening and where we at with this. Instead of just telling you. Know you now for yourself. Now. Know what I mean?"

"Of course, of course. But really – no, because that makes absolutely no sense. However, I think you are right, and I had supposed that you already knew everything," Bastard thanked him.

"I figured you'd figure it out. You're welcome. That's cool." Bastard and M.E. grinned at each other, though not necessarily for the same reason(s). "Before you keep thinking, let M.E. drop this. I know you'll pick it up easy."

"I'm listening."

"So keep listening. You know how risky it is for M.E. to be in the Nation. The word 'Eternal' means something, and that word legally technically qualifies my Exile status. Temporary Temporal Amnesty??? Fuck outta here. Don't mean shit to people who don't respect words. Shit could be revoked at any moment, for whatever. Could've already been revoked, they could be on their way to M.E. right now."

Bastard nodded empathetically and emphatically.

"Okay, my friend. Listen up: 'cause this is big. I didn't wanna start cookin' until I knew we had all the spices and enough spoons. But now – now, brother – now I can tell you. Son. We good."

Bastard couldn't think of anything more interesting to talk about.

M.E. proceeded, "What we got – we got something truly special, B. What really brings M.E. here. This'll impress you. We have a brand new motherfuckin' drug. A new drug!"

"Ha! A new drug??? Amazing." Bastard's excitement was apparent.

"Yeah man. That's what the man said. Something even you don't know about. A recent discovery – not yet recognized. This drug even targets a different part of the brain – receptors previously unidentified. Completely uncharted territory. So it can't be regulated by the Magistrates. No one knows about this shit. And this shit has been around forever, waiting for us to weigh it and move it. An unprecedented gift from our ever-providing and ever-fertile life-giving lovely Lady Dirt. None of this designer drug lab garbage. Old school. Botanical extraction. Plain and simple. Pure and natural, from the mountains in the jungle of the mountains. And it's ours."

Bastard's attempt at glee containment was futile. He leaned back in his chair to exhibit satisfaction, and I leaned back in mine.

"We know all the substances on the market today. We both have had, and still have, interests invested in these economies. One could say that we are balls deep in these areas."

Bastard and M.E. emptied their glasses of their contents. B refilled the vessels, and they cheered and drank again. He waited patiently in anticipation.

"I'm down South now, my brother. Lotta leaves growin' down there..."

"Hehehe," Bastard.

"Aight so. You remember Haile Leburik? The anthro-engineer? Author of *the Machine Compromise*?"

"Of course. That's my homie. I introduced you to him."

"Fuckin' of course, my bad. Ha. I always liked working with you, B. I missed you. For real for real."

"Missed you too, fam." They drank more.

"Leburik's also a bio-structural-chemico-botanico-engineer. No doubt you heard that he was Exiled, some Time ago..."

"Oh yeah, I think so – yeah. Happened when I was dead, right? Magistrates got our boy on Science charges. Something to do with his research – how alcohol moved through porous materials?"

"Yeah, pretty much. You know the cat. Genius progressed from analyzing the passage of water through soil to that of alcohols and gases through human skin. Apparently, the Nation doesn't approve of Science – unless they'd already approved of it as an appropriately approvable science. Ain't nothing new.

"Soon as the Magistrates realized that his work was leading to something that required further understanding, they mandated an Encounter. And you know from personal experience, brother – you know what an Encounter is, and you know that it has nothing do with playing chess. Point is, he was banished. So he came down to stay with M.E.."

"So you saying that Leburik found this new drug...?"

M.E. responded in the affirmative without moving.

"Jajaja, this is wonderful news! Dude, come on. How good is this noise?"

"Shit is amazing."

"Please, go on."

"Leburik calls it the White *Dove*. The flowers of the plant resemble – "

"The wings of a bleached pigeon?"

"What? No. The flowers of the plant look like a white dude diving. *Dove*. As in, past tense of dive. White is a noun, dove is a verb. The White *Dove*. I like it. You cool with it?"

"Of course, that's hilarious! Straight talk, Miguel, I was wondering about your pronunciation. And I'm down with that name, if only because nothing matters. But let me suggest: would you consider pronouncing it 'dove' like the bird, instead of '*dove*' like the past tense of dive? Cause birds fly, right? Suggests being high. Unless, wow! Unless this shit actually drives the melanin-deficient to seek out elevated precipices from which they are impelled to jump to their deaths? Hmm. I'll have to think about this some more..."

"You are incredibly odd. Nah, man. The drug does not inspire suicide by falling from a great height. Come on, dude. We're looking for repeat customers. Although, as always, I appreciate your misinterpretation, and you leave M.E. with new ideas. And I feel you on the phonetics. Nothing matters. And yes, birds do fly. So I'm down with saying the White Dove."

"Cool. So you've tried it?"

"Of course, Bastard. That's what brought M.E. here. That's why you're here. Our people have already begun harvesting." M.E. noticed a flash of concern on his friend's head-face. "Don't worry, man. They're well paid, well fed, well treated. You know how we do."

"Word. Thanks, sorry. Tell me more."

"I won't reveal exactly how beautiful the White Dove treats one. I had a bit prepared, but I'll skip it. You'll feel for yourself. Like I said, the White Dove operates on a unique and until now undiscovered part of the brain. It's not an alkaloid, nor does it hit serotonin, nor anymotherfuckingthing else officially mapped out and controlled by the Magistrates' National Committee of Neurologists and Neuroscientists and Neuroengineers of the Nationalized Nation (NCNNNNN). It works on a family of receptors presently unrecognized – and therefore prescriptively unregulated by the Nation and its Clock." M.E. paused for effect.

"We have our inside plant with your girl Des. We gotta figure out a way to get one of our guys into F-E 999's Neuro Transmission Center. And we have our friend tweak some shit, introduce a new radio emissions sequence that we've already designed, which targets those receptors that respond to the White Dove."

"Hold up, though," Bastard interrupted, ashamed. "We haven't installed our own receptors, though. So – "

"No need – don't have to! Mostly, the implants are installed to sell specific drugs that F-E 999 has designed – and some of them require the imposition of mechanico-neurological receptors. Now, our technology experts have devised a way for the White Dove waves to piggy-back, so to speak, on those lines that F-E 999 regularly broadcasts. When our transmission is received by a receptor with which it does not engage, the stimulus simply skips around the brain until it finds the right one."

"That's brilliant!"

"I know. And it's also untraceable. So this is it, B. This is our great little monster, our puppy, our horse's condom, our key to the lock on that door that opens for us to take other People's minds and balls.

"We'll set up a new company – using completely new pieces of paper and completely unexpected pens and pencils. We must be careful, and we must maintain operative compartmentalization, as usual, to protect the Organization's separate enterprises from sweeping Magisterial Scrutiny.

"And we'll make mad balls. More balls than anyone could ever need. Only issue is that we gotta accomplish everything by Pre-Centerday. That's when I'm being shipped home, the day after Wonderday, according to theM."

M.E. breathed. "So. What should we call our new company? Oh shit, before I forget, here's the product that we're producing and pushing. On M.E.." Their palms met under the table for a hand-off. "Start off light – this should be a few doses for you. And that's accounting for your experience and expertise."

"Ah, thank you, Miguel! Very excited to taste this. What a treat!" Bastard eagerly accepted an oversized glycine bag containing what Bastard estimated to be about one gram. "How about Orange Vulture, Inc.?"

"It's okay with M.E." and raised his glass. "Cheers, motherfucker. To old friends."

"To the Organization."

"To the White Dove."

9

PERHAPS NOT DESERVING OF ITS OWN CHAPTER.

Bastard felt good, lifted. He floated his way back to the office with ease. The White Dove intrigued him, and he was very eager to get home and try it.

XERXES DAY (THREE)

BASTARD GETS ANOTHER PHONE CALL.

That's what woke him up. The next day. He wasn't used to phone calls, and the rings that rang repeatedly displeased him.

He got out of bed and kinda rushed his post-somnambulatory practices, increasingly motivated by a need to silence that awful two-eared broken calculator.

By the time he sat down in the chair behind his desk, the phone decided to stop ringing. Bastard appreciated this moment of silence, but feared that the ringing would recommence. And he was right. He lifted the hand-to-ear-piece.

"—" Bastard couldn't think of something to say.

"Hello? Hello?"

"Thank you, and hello."

"This is the seventh time I'm calling – I've been desperately trying to reach you."

"Great! I'm happy for your success. I must ask, though: who is this 'you' that you speak of? And who are you, you?"

"Are you Detective Bastard?"

"Is that who the first 'you' is?"

"Detective Bastard???" the voice asserted forcefully.

"Bastard."

"Fuck you," came the nasal retort. Then, "Oh. I see. Just Bastard. My name is Lance Newcomb. I have a company called Free-Enterprise 999. I'd like to meet with you."

Bastard didn't hesitate. "Sure, yeah. Come to my office."

"I don't know where that is."

"If I tell you where it is, will you then come?"

"Yes," Newcomb replied truthfully.

"Okay," and Bastard announced his address.

He hung up the phone and walked back over to the bedroom adjacent, where he regarded Curiosity. She lay still, still sleeping on the floor bed. Her beautiful skin and voluptuous thick black hair made her violent snoring tolerable, even cute.

Though he had no memories of hooking up with her the previous night, her presence comforted him. After some thought, he shook his head and returned to the office and his chair.

Soft gray powder appeared mauve upon the brown surface of his desk. About half a gram of the White Dove randomly sprawled across before him. He must have spilled some out last night?

Bastard scraped the powder into one tiny mountain. With very little consideration, he rolled up a small piece of paper and blasted near half of the half gram into his right nostril, after which he ventured into a brief mental constitutional.

BASTARD GETS A JOB!?!

Suspiciously soon, the rapping of bare knuckles pleading at the front door interrupted Bastard's slumped slumber.

He lifted his head from its desk. I could see that he was both excited and nervous, because I could see him.

Curiosity had awoken. She stood in the doorless doorway between the bedroom and the office, unclothed and quietly radiant. With sleep-eyes she asked him why he was already up. Bastard stood up and approached her. They embraced. The knuckles hit the door again.

"Oh yeah. I mean, Yes, I'm coming." He waved Curiosity back into the bedroom and sat back down.

I rose to my feet and opened the door. A tall, poorly dressed man in very expensive but ill-fitting attire entered the room and said, "Bastard. I am Lance Newcomb."

Bastard assessed the man before addressing him.

Lance Newcomb inhabited an aged but ageless figure

that was slender but jagged, with a forward-jutting upper body. He was thin but wide-framed, like a flattened cardboard box. There seemed to exist a lot of space between his chalky gray skin and his clothes, which appeared to float around his body rather than fall fittingly. Imposing facial features informed an unfortunate physiognomy that offered a promise of forthcoming unpleasantness; his protruding proboscis appeared to be rotting.

His physical form could not but insert itself. Walking like a clothes hanger that can walk towards a desk, the man advanced. Bastard knew, although he kind of knew before, that he wasn't going to like this guy.

I closed the office door, which startled Newcomb. He twisted around and, seeing nothing, even more quickly snapped back to face Bastard. But for one split second, I saw his face, divided into eight like some pie.

"Oh, yeah?" Bastard stared hard and long at the man, which was very awkward. Then he laughed and got up. "I'm just fucking around, man. Yes, welcome. Have that seat."

The tall man sat down. "I'm not in a joking mood, Detective."

"Bastard is fine," sitting. "What can I do for you?"

Lance Newcomb heavily heaved a huff. Then he slapped open palms on his thighs, just above the knees. "Well, ... all right. Can I ask you a question?"

"You just did."

"Okay, you're a smartass. I get it. Can I ask you a question or not?"

"Yes! And we both know that you can. We've already established that."

"You're an utter jackass."

Bastard agreed with a smile. He was starting to feel

better, which prompted the realization that he had felt worse earlier.

"All right then," Lance grumbled. "*May* I ask you a question?"

"Another one? Fucking hell. Just kidding, of course you may. I just hope that you learned your lesson."

"You are exhausting."

"And exhaustive. Drink?"

"Yes please," Newcomb shoveled out in larded exasperation. This was neither interesting nor fun.

Bastard reached into a drawer and brought out a bottle of grain, the same one he'd put away sometime earlier for some reason he had thought was good at the Time but could now no longer remember, and two glasses. He filled the latter with part of the contents of the former, then handed his visitor one of the glasses. I remained standing in the far corner of the room, observing their interaction as if I wasn't there.

Bastard tilted his glass towards the old man and took a perfunctory sip off the top. "So...what's your fucking question?"

"All right, Mister – Detective – Bastard. Here's the deal. I own a company called Free-Enterprise 999. Ever heard of it?"

"Wait, what? That's your question?"

"What is the matter with you?"

"Was that your original question? Or?"

Lance's pallid face-flesh now looked rouged. Bastard was exceedingly pleased with himself. Yes, he enjoyed being an asshole; and this routine had purpose.

"Do you talk to all of your clients this way?"

"Actually..." Bastard didn't have to think long to answer the question, because he hadn't any clients. "Actually...yes... I mean, yes, I do. Go on."

"Right. Of course. I know that you placed an order

with our licensed pharmaceutical distribution center, for a gross gross of dilaudid," Newcomb mumbled with uncertain authority. His small deep dark eyes darted around the small room nervously while he compulsively rubbed his palms up and down his thighs.

I knew it was an act, and so did Bastard. But what role was he performing here, for whom and for what? Lance Newcomb was at the top of the criminal overworld food chain, which means that he could eat everything, but nothing could eat him. Popular belief placed Lance Newcomb as the Grand Vampire; whether or not that was true, he was unquestionably one of the most powerful sentient beings alive. He had no reason to be anxious before a systematically incarcerated, tortured, killed, previously dead, and generally ill-regarded peasant shit-starter pariah like Bastard.

Assuming that this meeting was a set-up, Bastard proceeded to prod for clues by continuing to play his own game.

Newcomb resumed, "You did get the, uh, the dilau – "

"Dude, what the fuck?" Bastard seemed to react. "This isn't some customer service courtesy call. And it's not a social visit because even though we've never met, we strongly dislike each other. Can we do this?"

"I have to apologize...I'm not used to these types of situations..." his voice skedaddling at the end. I watched his words disperse in random directions.

"That's okay, Mr. Creeper-Man." Newcomb did not like this new nickname, which helped Bastard smile again. "Your business ain't none of my business, unless you choose to make it your business to make your business my business. If you feel it, tell me what's on your purportedly ancient dome-piece, and perhaps we can secure a more productive conversation." Bastard leaned back in his chair and sparked a bone. Thrilled to practice his private dick jive with a real-life client, he smoked with complete and utter disregard for whatever the shit was gonna be the shit of this shituation.

"Are you gonna let me speak my fucking piece – " Lance Newcomb faltered, half-expecting Bastard to say something crude, rude, inflammatory, unhelpful. But Bastard knew how to keep playing, and kept quiet. Newcomb was thrown by Bastard's sudden silence and apparent attentiveness. He resumed, "I think someone may be trying to take me."

"Take you where, sir?" Bastard couldn't resist.

"To rob me, to blackmail me, to fuck me and my business, you dolt!" the old man slobberingly stammered.

"I see," said Bastard, unfazed by Newcomb's verbal attack. "Listen, I'm sorry about that last one. I'm getting tired of this, too. I don't like to repeat myself; it is tiresome and very un-motherfucking-lady-like, for myself. Please tell me what you want, because I'd rather you leave sooner than later. Cool?"

Newcomb groaned.

Bastard downed his drink and took two last drags off his smoke before extinguishing it in the over-crowded blue opal ashtray. "Cool, then. Please, go on. For real for real."

"I own a very important, very profitable, highly specialized company, sir,"

"Of questionable legality, sir,"

"And I have 3D video surveillance everywhere in the complex,"

"As you should,"

"And I was reviewing last night's tapes this morning,"

"Naturally,"

"NOT naturally. Will you stop parroting me? It's not

natural. I don't often review the security footage. I'm not a paranoid person."

"Maybe you should be," Bastard shot back, unsure of whether Newcomb meant that he was not paranoid or not a person.

"Indeed," the old man mused. "Perhaps." Again – a person?

"So? What did you see, on those tapes, that has brought you to my offices today?"

"Office."

"Fair enough."

"My wife."

"Your wife, sir?"

"Yes, my wife."

"Oh cool! And who was she – I mean, what was she doing?"

"Not amused."

"Thanks. Not sorry."

"Whatever. My wife was in the NTC last night... – the Neuro Transmission Center – with one of my top technical engineers, the Extraordinary Ordinator of the Ordinateur, Evgren Todorowsky. And this asshole is showing her how we transmit neo-narcotic neuro-radio-wave stimuli to our customers."

"Haha."

"What's funny?"

"You said customers. That's fucking funny. Go on."

"No one is allowed in the NTC – not even the two guys who run the dissemination colors – except for Todorowsky. He's not allowed out of the NTC, either. In fact, I never built a door for the NTC, to ensure that no one could ever get in or out. But somehow, she got in there. And I want to know how; I want to know what she's up to, because she's definitely up to something. I

need you to find out for me – what is that something."
Newcomb seemed to be sincere.

"I see. That doesn't sound right. How long have you known your wife?"

"Four hundred large rotations."

"Hm. Has she ever tried to pull anything on you in the past? Threaten you or your business interests? Sleep with someone else?"

"What? No. She can sleep with whomever she wants, that's not it. Only reason we're still together after all this Time."

"Well, maybe it was a weird Machine Compromise kind of sex thing. You probably have nothing to worry about. Maybe she's working on a birthday surprise for you."

Newcomb leered. "I don't have a birthday, and even if I did, you're still not funny. This is a critical breach of protocol and trust. There is no good reason why she would be in my NTC!" he awkwardly exclaimed rabidly, then tried to regain his composure. "I wanna know how she got in there – and why."

He pulled the chair in closer, his skeletal knees almost hitting the desk but not – though he flinched slightly as if they had. "Even if you are a junkie," he seethed through his teeth, "I know you're not stupid. And I know your story. Have some respect for your elders."

"You're right, I'm not stupid. Disagree on the respect thing, though. Seems arbitrary – age – numbers, I mean. Fuck off – I'm older than death." Bastard decided that he no longer wanted to continue talking. "Look dude, this is already a boring memory. I listened to your story. No idea what it has to do with M.E.. My advice? Divorce your scheming wife and hire a more trustworthy Ordinarily Ordained Ordinance Ordinator. What do you want me to do about it?"

"I'm hiring you to follow my wife. I'm giving you a job, you ass." Newcomb expressed the last sentence with his greatest contempt thus far. He histrionically slapped a large envelope on the desk. "Here's a file on her."

He stood up and walked out of the room before Bastard could ask him why he had a file on his own wife, and tell him that he wasn't hiring clients at the moment.

12

IN WHICH THE PLOT THICKENS WITH THE ADDITION OF A NEW INGREDIENT.

The door announced its closure. The air within began to settle and relax. Nothing moved.

Bastard waited for the envelope to say something. When he was sure that it would never talk, he picked it up, opened it, and turned it upside down.

The envelope had contained two items, both of which were now on his desk. And although both items had already been on his desk, this was the first time they were directly touching its surface. He set it back down, wanting to think that he had achieved a major victory in the fight for equality. Then he realized how silly that sounded. He crumpled up the envelope and threw it in the garbage, as the two newly liberated items cheered. He had brought about the end of their captor's reign. Bastard was a hero.

One of them was a flat sphere of five thousand balls. The other one was a photograph of Lance Newcomb's wife.

Bastard grabbed his balls and put them in (one of) his drawers, after which his gaze unconsciously rested at Newcomb's drink. The fact that the glass hadn't moved since its initial placement bothered Bastard. But the glass had not come from the envelope.

Upon refocusing his attention on the photo of Mrs. Newcomb before him, Bastard abruptly splattered a sputtered laugh from the depths of his spleen. Then he shrugged in appreciation. Quick and true, as if saying, "Holy shit that's hilarious! No shit. Ha!"

Although he had never seen a picture of this woman before, he immediately recognized her. And though the possibility had never occurred to him, Bastard was not surprised to learn that Newcomb's wife was his new girl from the place – Despi.

But he was amused, if unpleasantly.

13

HUH.

The hydromorphone pills were small and easily finely crushable. Satisfied with the consistency of the powder, he set down his briquette and reflected upon how the fruit of his labor would taste. After very little thought, he added the rest of the White Dove and mixed the combination.

Next, he took a cigarette from a pack that contained other cigarettes. He rolled it between two of his most useful fingers, loosening the tobacco before dumping some of it out. This also made it easier for Bastard to remove the filter, which he ripped apart and replaced half of.

Cigarette in mouth, he bent his head close to the desk and sucked some of the powder up into it. Then he twisted the top of the cigarette paper to close it. Before lighting up, he inhaled the remaining majority of the powder through a nostril.

Bastard leaned back in his chair, White Dove-opiate coolie between his lips. Very carefully he lighted up and motionlessly toked, holding in the smoke, sipping his drink, coughing, thinking, *Why was Des inside the NTC last night? She's supposed to go there today... Why did she go yesterday, for what reason? Will she level? And will she go again tonight? Also, why did Lance Newcomb come here? To hire a private detective to tail his wife, or to let me know that Despi's his wife? What could be gained by this play – and whose play is it? Are they working together? Or against each other? And how the fuck is Des over four hundred years old?*

When the coolie died, he held his other hand under its long dead ash and carried it to bury it in the blue opal 'shtray.

Two things about this case bothered him. One was the fact that Lance Newcomb hadn't tasted his drink. Bastard reached over, grabbed it, poured the booze into his mouth, and leaned back in his chair.

He awoke a circle or two later, slowly lifting his head from its position on his arm on his desk. He noticed a new burn on his forearm, which made no sense.

The Circhronometer mumbled, "Ninety."

"I didn't ask," Bastard spat. He drank what little was left in his glass. Then he stood up, gathered most of himself, and headed out to see M.E..

14

THE MECHANIC IS ALIVE!!!

Bastard arrived at the bar, hoping his partner in crime might be there already. M.E. wasn't, of course. M.E. was always on time, exactly on time, all the time, no matter what time it was, even if it wasn't.

Sitting at the table, he worked at his highballs carefully, thinking the situation over: I have the most brilliant criminologist in the world putting me to work. I have a beautiful woman working for me on the inside. And I've just been hired, finally, as a detective, by the very man we're trying to take. It's too perfect – something's not right. It's funny how the stirrer bends below the plane of the liquid in a glass. It's somewhat otherworldly, and slightly unsettling. I wish it wouldn't do that. But something's not right. M.E., Des, Newcomb. What do these three people want from me? What am I getting myself into here?

"Oh hey," Bastard started at the scraping of chair legs. "What time is it?" dazed.

"Eleven twenty-ten zero. What's 'a matter?" Miguel sat down.

"Nothing." Bastard shook himself up, coming to, regaining ultimate awareness. "Cool. We got half a circle before Despi shows up. What's happening? How was the session?"

"What?"

"Court?"

"Oh yeh," M.E. laughed. "I met with some of the lawyers today, almost half of them, if I counted right. Supposed to meet some more later today, so I'll count again. But everything went fine today. It's a really nice feeling to simultaneously be on the level with the ones who want to control you while playing them like a pool shark at a dive bar full of wannabe players. I sank every pocket. I sank the eight-ball before they even had a chance to chalk their sticks."

"I can't believe you played billiards with them."

"Yeh, it's ridiculous, I know. But that's what they're doing these days." M.E. smiled. "So far so good. I can't wait to testify against Newt Humbert. That guy really has it coming! Unfortunately, it's hard to find his current address, or any updated information on his whereabouts."

"I still don't understand what you're doing here, really," Bastard wondered. "In the Nation, I mean. Why you're testifying against someone we don't know for doing something that you done did yourself, after you were banned. You know we don't fuck with their courts."

"Oh, I thought it was clear, my bad. See, I'd already begun spreading rumors about Newt Humbert before I got Exiled. It was a set-up for another plan that I was working on at the Time, well before my Encounter. But that plan got foiled. So instead, I dropped Newt Humbert's name as being responsible for the Guns and

Butter Scandal..." M.E.'s eyes scanned askance for any wayward glance. Even though no one was listening, he lowered his voice to say, "How I was able to pull off that heist, brother, after having been Exiled... – even just getting back into the Nation on the low-low – and then getting out... It's too long of a tale to tell you in this moment.

"And so I waited for the right reason to resurrect him. Leburik's discovery of the White Dove led to the realization of the meaning of life for Mr. Newt "Newt" Humbert. I sent the Magistrates a postcard that Newt Humbert had come to see M.E. in my village in the South. Story goes that he was honored that I'd given him the Time of day, which, after consulting my watch, happened to be forty-six. To make up for my graciousness, he shared with M.E. the details of the Guns and Butter joint. Being a citizen of the Nation who wishes to make amends for past mistakes, I simply performed a National duty by passing the information along to the Magistrates. And I told them that I'd be happy to testify against him."

"But who the fuck is – ?"

"Are you daft? I am Newt Humbert. Newt Humbert is M.E.. Damn, dude. Was that not clear?"

"Eh," Bastard shrugged.

"Well, now you know, and now you know that you know. All good. What's up with you?"

"Oh! I got a job today."

"What? Someone hired your ass to do some detective work? Didn't they check your record?"

They both laughed; Bastard relaxed, remembering who he was – where he was, who he was with, what he was doing, what he was doing there with his oldest, longest, most trusted friend. "Yeh, yeh. Right? It's ludicrous. But it's even more so! Get this: my client?

Lance Newcomb. My job? Tail-job. Tailing? His wife. His wife? Despi Belle."

"Wow."

"Yeh."

"Nice."

"Yeh."

"Does she know?"

"Nope – at least, not from my side. Not sure."

"Good. Don't tell her. Not yet, at least."

"Wasn't planning on it."

"Of course you weren't." Miguel smiled. At that moment, Despi's face appeared in the doorway. M.E. felt the air change behind him (Bastard had agreed to watch his back) as she opened the door and walked in. Turning his head, his eyes settled on her approaching body; then M.E. turned back to Bastard, who was himself refocused on this distraction.

"Not this one, Jim," I think I heard him mutter beneath his breath as she traversed the floor towards our table, although I could be wrong. He rose to make introductions. "M.E., I'd like you to meet Despi'kha Belle. Des, may I present to you, Miguel Evangelista."

M.E. stood up, presenting the hand at the end of his extended right arm that presently met a hand of Des. I'd bet that neither of them had shared an equal, "A pleasure, I'm sure," as they'd chosen to agree. Their skin gloves hugged and their arms wagged up and down.

The clock spoke, "Midnight," but softly in our ears.

Everyone sat down.

We waited in silence as the waitress took Despi's order. Then we waited in silence for several some more. Bastard began again only after her drink arrived. At which point they cheered, cordially, and then, "M.E. is the brains before and behind and under and on top of this operation," he tossed about directly. Looking at his friend, "Des is Agent Alien in this operation. Pleasantries completed, let us begin." Everyone sat down again once more.

"Do we know how to break into the Neuro Transmission Center? Have you talked with the Ordinateur Ordinator?"

"Yes, and it went well. His name's Evgen Todorowsky. I teased him into showing me around the NTC – tonight, after hours. Seems easy enough to get into, considering there's no door. Only issue is, they have security cameras running all night."

Only M.E. and I could notice the unnoticeable flash in Bastard's eyes. And I don't know if M.E. noticed it.

In Bastard's head he wondered, *Why didn't Des say that she was in the NTC last night? Why is she holding out on M.E.?*

Then he thought quietly without words; and then he thought, *Hell. If she's gonna play that, then she must not know that her husband, Newcomb, is playing it, too.*

"The cameras won't be an issue," Bastard carried on. "And you'll meet our man, he'll be here soon."

"Who we sendin' in?"

"The Mechanic, of course."

"I thought he died."

"Did he? I didn't know that. Anyway, he'll be here -" Bastard stopped talking, for he saw the man enter and stood up to greet him.

The Mechanic introduced himself to Des; and he and Miguel Evangelista paid each other respect. He's cool like that. The Mechanic always had respect; he always showed love. This is very important to the Organization. And as a member of the Organization – and as a lovely person – the Mechanic knew that this mattered.

The four of them sat and drank together.

And then they drank some more, so as to talk.

Bastard brought it back after a bit. "So yeh, Des, don't worry about the cameras. And dude – they got triple D live surveillance mad eyes in the sky, as expected. Just a confirmation."

"Bet," said Macchine – the Mechanic. (My bad.)

Everyone nodded in accord.

"Everything is set, then."

Miguel picked it up to wrap it. "Tonight, after the job is done, I'd like for the four of us to meet here. Tomorrow morning, we will all – everyone involved in this project – we will all meet at the Loam. If anything happens and you can't make it tonight – tomorrow morning at the Loam." M.E. turned his head and looked upward. He releveled and continued, "I'd like to catch up tonight, but tomorrow's meeting is much more important. When we're in the Loam, we're under the grid. So don't take any unnecessary risks."

M.E. stood up and said his peace out-revoirs before leaving.

"You know what you are to do, and you know when and where," Bastard tried to seal.

"Whereat the – " the Mechanic –

– " – Yeh, whereat the Loam be tomorrow?" Despi finished.

"Even the Organization can't personally touch all three suns on the low!" Bastard looked to make a knowing HAHA! chuckle grin, even though he knew that M.E. had already bounced, and there would be no reflection. He continued, "Aight. Y'all already know that no one knows where the Loam is until it is there, where it is? You'll know when we know. If not tonight, then tomorrow morning, you will know.

"So," he stood up and pushed the chair back in under the table. "Are we good? Everyone cool, right?" Instead of waiting for their nods, he walked up to the bar, where he asked to use the phone.

He pressed some buttons before coughing, "Yeh, this is Bastard," into it. "Newcomb? Yeh, come to my office, I have something for you. I'll be there in a bit. Just come after you close up, that's fine."

Des and the Mechanic went off to talk about shit. Bastard headed home.

15

WHAT YOU SEE IS WHAT YOU GET.

A big man in a blue baseball cap with the letter C stitched on the front in red thread walked down the sidewalk in front of Bastard's building, thirty-three levels beneath his office window.

Minutes later, the man was walking back up the street, in the other direction. He was making an effort to appear relaxed but on schedule, as if clearly going somewhere.

Apparently, Bastard's place was being watched.

Colors of used cars, a super hosing down the walk, the occasional fake bird soaring inside the sky; and the sounds of engines running, a truck beeping backing up, a whistle, people vocalizing – none of this could puncture the eerie aura of controlled projected stillness and quietness in the air of the area.

Bastard waited for some certain impending complication. He understood that although people and animals and machines can lie, air can never conceal or avoid truth; it exists only in a state of pure honesty (otherwise it is not air, or it does not exist). Every subtlety before him commanded great attention in suspicion of potential significance. In a silent imposition, the slightest vibration could prove deafening.

A large greenish-gray van drove up the block and stopped across from the man in the blue cap, who was now standing in front of Bastard's place. Blue cap nodded and crossed the street, as two men emerged from the van's torso. He said some words to them and got in the van, which then drove away.

The two new guys almost got hit by a car as they made their way from the middle of the street to the front door of Bastard's building, which they entered.

Bastard took a few minutes to finish his drink. Then he paid his tab, left the little bar across the street from his place, and followed the two guys in.

16

IN WHICH BASTARD HOSTS A PIG ROAST.

"What's up, assholes?" Bastard closed the door behind him. The sound startled Officer Ottoman, who was going through the drawers of Bastard's desk. "Fuck you looking for? I may be able to help, you know. I put most of this stuff here..."

"Shut up, low-life," Officer Rosalito had stopped rummaging around the adjacent bedroom to step into the office. "We'll ask the questions. And if we want help, we'll ask that, too."

Curiosity must have left, cause she's one to fight, and Bastard had heard no sound of a scuffle. Bastard couldn't resist but to ask them another question. "So, what do you guys want?"

"That's more like it," Ottoman said.

Bastard was confused.

"You've been seen being cheeky with Miguel Evangelista. Regularly. Now you tell us about that."

"That's not even a question. I'm gonna sit down, in

that my chair," he pointed, directing the oafish officer out of his way.

"Start talking."

"Listen, M.E.'s an old friend. You know that. And regularly? He's only been here two days." Bastard evicted a cigarette from its home.

"Old friend, huh? Do all your friends send you up the river for a four and six?"

"Only did three and seven," Bastard smiled, lighting the cigarette. "Got out early...good behavior." He waved the match dead.

"We heard. How'd you land that? Boning the prison warden is what they told us." Ottoman and Rosalito laughed their pudgy wax faces gross, very easily amused. They were both simple men; ignorant, sensitive, stupid, and armed. Their laughter was like carbon monoxide – senseless, fatal.

"That's right, Ottoman. I never knew your mother ran that prison. She ain't bad, either. But from what I hear, you already know that sauce, fat man."

"You little fucker," he reached out and hit Bastard across the face with a clenched fist that held even more anger in it.

Bastard hurt. Still seated, he bent over slowly, picked up his cigarette from down on the floor, and laid it dead in the ashtray.

Rosalito reached for a bottle of pills on the desk. "Still on the shit, huh?" he said, disgusted. Bastard cringed at the cop's oral wind, for his breath stank like a pile of steaming freshly made pig shit.

"It helps me deal with pain of looking at your faces. Anyway, Fuck you, it's all legal. I got a script."

"It's illegal?"

"I said, 'all legal.' You know that's what I said."

"All right, enough pussy-footing. What's Evangelista up to?"

"Come off it, Ottoman." He loved being able to say that, so he couldn't not smile. "He's here to testify for your employers against Newt Humbert in the Guns and Butter Affair. Do you like hearing what you already know? Or are you just terribly forgetful? Ask again in a few minutes – I really hate to repeat myself, but I'll do it for the children."

"If you don't spill it, we may just have to take you in," sneered Rosalito as awfully as he could, though the sound slumped silly on the floor.

"On what charges, fuckfacers? You're wasting your time. I'm gonna have a drink. You want one? I'm guessing it be a slow day on the streets. You know it's funny, we've known each other for so long, and we've never really hung out before. Let's have a drank – please, sit down – one of you, take that chair, the other you can sit on the fucking floor. Would you like a glass or did you bring a trough?"

"Let's go, Ott. This deadbeat ain't worth shit."

Such trite dialogue excited Bastard, who now kinda wanted them to stay.

"We're watching you," he continued, leaning over the desk, his hands on the edge, his fingers curled and pressing up beneath the slight ledge that extended just beyond the body and upper thighs of the legs of the desk. "I'm itching to put you back inside where you belong." Bastard heard Rosalito's forearm muscles twitch through a shirtsleeve as he pressed the fingers of his right hand up underneath against the ledge. Rosalito pushed himself off the desk and took two steps away, smiling.

"I don't know if that's where I belong, really, but if Ottoman's mom is itching inside where he belongs, I might be able to scratch it for her, for him. Unless you mean inside the ground, cause I think I do belong there, and I liked being dead more than in prison."

Ottoman could no longer hold back his red ire and lunged at Bastard. He got two rough hits in before Rosalito restrained him. The air settled, then it settled enough to speak a few.

"Thanks, Rosie-baby. I owe you one. Dinner tomorrow? My place or yours?"

"Go fuck yourself," and the two uninvited guests left, the last one slamming the door behind him. Bastard was happy to see them go. So happy that he did, in fact, fuck himself. He thought about Curiosity – and then he thought about Des.

After, Bastard stayed in his chair. He poured himself that glass that Ottoman and Rosalito had so callously refused. He took some in. Then he got up, walked to the front of his desk, bent down, ripped off the bug that Rosalito had affixed under the ledge, opened the window and threw it outside. He left the window open and sat back down. He could hear the engines and the wheels of auto machines down there on the streets below, working.

The phone rang and Bastard answered it right away.

"Hey, I got you! You're getting good at this, brother," M.E. marked.

"Ha!" Bastard made some smiles. "Yeh."

"So whattup man?"

"Chilling, man. Waiting for Newcomb right now. Got the windows open, airing out the stank of pork in my office."

"What – you having a barbecue or something? I'm,a roll up!" M.E. jested.

"Fuck off. What's goin' on?"

"Change of plans. We're to meet tonight in the

basement of Quinine. Same time. Inform the others."
M.E. hung up.

Bastard sat still and waited for the next sounds.

17

A HEALTHY VOLLEY, TO WASTE TIME.

The next sound to arrive was one that Bastard both expected and recognized. The rap of familiar knuckles upon his hinged doorframe insertion prompted him to shout, "Yeh. Come in."

"Well, Mr. Detective Mr. Man," Lance Newcomb's voice dripped with sagging thick despite as he slinked through the space. "What do you have?"

"First of all, tall gray gaunt old man, I'd appreciate it if you adopted if not a kinder, then at least a more professional, tone of voice when you fucking talk to me: Bastard."

Having pronounced his own name, Bastard felt better.

"I am in no mood for games, Detective Mister Bastard. I am concerned solely with the welfare of my business."

"And being in the employ of your fine business, Mr. Newcomb Man, I recommend that you may ... indeed, I believe that you will achieve better results from

Detective Mister Man's services by not addressing him with utter contempt."

Newcomb's cheeks flushed a rosy hue that might have been pretty were it not gracing a rather ugly man's withered gray-white dry skin. "I don't really beg your pardon. I detest drug addicts."

"As I detest pushers, I'm sure," Bastard was having fun with this conversation. "It's a common model in such relationships. In fact, this tendency is typical in consumer-supplier relations, and it has always been of great interest to M.E.."

"I am not a pusher, I am a legitimate businessperson-man," Newcomb menaced. His exhibition of severe displeasure turned effrontery seemed excessive – hyperbolic, over the top, exaggerated; a bit too much. After all, why should he be so resentful of the pathetic motherfuckers whose weaknesses, upon which he preyed for profit, afforded his luxury apartments and his luxurious luxuries? But this change of tactic, the alteration of his behavior...for he presented a completely different man than the one who had first visited the office...fascinated Bastard, who was compelled to wonder about the purpose of this random transformation from stuttering coward to smarmy condescending twat. "But to state my regard for you more directly," Lance Newcomb asserted, "I simply detest you. It's only personal."

"Listen, ass – don't chip at my clip. I'm trying to tell you some shit that's important. You think I give a hit about your whip? Newcomb, please. Consider yourself lucky that I'm not into blackmail, cause I'm talking about some pressing juice. What I will give, if you fucking listen, is what you paid for."

Newcomb blinked, and then tried not to blink again. He was of a very old school, in which blinking was taught to be a sign of weakness. This belief was eventually dismissed in favor of a higher logic that proved that any effort to conceal perceptible weakness was in itself a greater show of vulnerability. That's how old Lance Newcomb was.

Bastard went on.

"Earlier today, early after the third noon, your wife left F-E 999's main headquarters and met with Evgen Todorowsky – the Ordained Ordination dude who, according to the tapes which you never offered to produce, showed her around the NTC last night. Anyway, I watched them for some Time, but was unable to attract any light from their meeting. They were dining at a gourmet restaurant, and it was fully booked. I was denied a table. Following the meal, for which she paid, they parted ways – amicably, not romantically, and with an air of confidential camaraderie. Then your wife proceeded, and I followed her – both of us on foot.

"She arrived at a bar around first midnight where she met with two men. The three spoke for about half an hour. Unfortunately, I couldn't catch most of their conversation since I had to take the utmost care in not being noticed. After that -"

"Who were these men?" Newcomb peeved. "Could you determine at the very least the nature of their meeting?"

"Man, I was at the other end of the bar! I'm new at this. But my eyes are pretty good, and so are my lip-reading skills. The one man was introduced as Frances Tournedor – he was dark skinned and looked good. Didn't catch the other guy's name, but he seemed mad cool. Both sounded official, and they acted organized. They spoke very little to each other. Very little. Like probably less than you and she talk. Anyway, it was clear that she had never met these two – individually, or together.

"I ran the name Frances Tournedor through all of the criminals' databases (we have a bunch). Nothing. The only match for that name is in the jaundiced pages – appears he's a successful uptown corporate lawyer with a high price tag. I'll look him up tomorrow, pay him a free visit. Depending on the company's returns policy, I may try to take him out, bring him downtown. I'm hoping that this lead will lead to the next."

Lance Newcomb was visibly displeased with the story, which made Bastard happy. He continued, "The fancy man left first; then your wife left with the other dude. I followed them until they split up. Then she met up with E. T. again. Then I called you."

"You're utterly useless. Why did you call? This isn't information."

"Not nothing now, what?" Bastard splat. "It's pretty fucking clear, old man."

"What?"

"Your wife is a serial adulterer. Sometimes with more than one party a day, sometimes with more than one party at a time; sometimes both and twice and both twice in one day – if not more."

"What are you on about, Bastard?"

"Can't you see? I followed your wife for half a day – during which she hooked up with three different dudes three different times, and one time was with two dudes."

"I want pictures of these men," Lance pressed his words through his teeth, straining.

"Sure, man. And I want that footage of your girl and E.T. in the NTC last night. Can we meet up tomorrow? 'Cause I gotta pick up the film first, it's being developed right now – not right now, because the store closes overnight. Anyway, the photos will be ready tomorrow. You bring the tape, and we'll swap."

Newcomb ignored this. "What next?"

"What? Oh. Next. I don't know what I thought I heard you say. Way I see it, you have a few options: fire that guy and give your wife the boot. You should do both either way. Change all your passwords and reboot the system, and lock up the shop better. Actually, you should do that anyway." He paused, suddenly pleased. "This is surprisingly good advice! I am confident that if you do these things, you will have lost nothing more than you already would have. And I'd be willing to bet that, five or ten Cycles from now, this problem of yours will be remembered as a minor blip in an otherwise successful career (radar scan career assessment result). Something to joke about with your clan, if not with your future five-hundred-year old wife."

He hesitated before saying the following, but figured it would be worth seeing how Newcomb would react: "Honestly, Lance Newcomb Man, as much as I appreciate your balls, I don't believe you have any further need of my services."

Newcomb shifted as if lightly pinched. He reached into a pocket and glanced at a message on his personal handheld data transmission module. He quickly put it in his pants and looked up at Bastard. "Yes, yes. I guess maybe you're right. Thank you." And he rose to his feet.

Too easy, Bastard thought. Strange. Why did Newcomb acquiesce so readily? Bastard had expected an argument from his client, or at least some hostile indignation...instead, Newcomb agreeably accepted his tender resignation. Why? Why did Newcomb think he was done here – what had been accomplished by their independently co-produced charade? What was that message that Newcomb had just received – who sent it, what did it say?

"Well, we can't thank you enough, Bastard. How much do we owe you for your incredibly helpful work? Do you take checks?"

"I prefer cash balls, mister," Bastard smiled. "Tax purposes."

"I thought you had died – you still have to pay taxes after you die?"

"Even in death, man. Fucked up, right?" It was odd to share a human moment with his nemesis. "Considering I didn't do anything, you don't owe me, ma'am. Actually, if anything, I owe you change for that five thousand balls you gave me yesterday – but I don't have it. Let's call it square then? Happy Day – that's what you say, right?"

Newcomb produced and offered another five hundred balls, which Bastard accepted; they shook hands and the man left.

Bastard checked the Circhronometer, which showed 15:3.

Go change your passwords, creeper, he thought to himself. It's okay with M.E.... We're already in.

But something just ain't right, right? Again, what was that message about? And why that extra five hundy – was it some kind of buy-off bonus payment? Leave it alone?

As he sat there pondering Newcomb's unexpectedly abrupt and generous departure, Bastard fashioned himself a special smoke and drifted off for a couple of circles. He had much to process. It had been a long day, and it wasn't over yet.

18

AFTER-DINNER DRINKS.

The four of them met that night in the basement of Quinine: Miguel Evangelista, Despi, the Mechanic, and Bastard.

The sub-level of this bar was one of their old haunts – before Miguel Evangelista was Exiled, before the first time Bastard left. The space provided some security: it was underground, it was dark, it was dingy, it was discreet, it was dislocated, it was dangerous. There were five large empty old wine barrels, each big enough for a table and chairs for up to six or eight heads. Back in the day, Bastard and M.E. used to get high there.

Our two heroes were the first to arrive by about ten, intentionally; they crawled into their old barrel in the rear and sat at the little table within.

"So I talked to the owner of the other bar," Miguel opened. "You know how they do – "

"Yeh."

"And you know that because we – "

"Yeh."

"So dude came up to M.E. on the street – gave word that the place was bugged. Right after our last meeting, they got a visit from the Anti-Exterminator."

"Fuck off."

"No joke. Anyway, it's good to have friends. And these cats here, this place – they'll likewise let us know if anything."

"Right."

"Yo – what's up with your roast, man? You still grillin'?"

"Very good. Our old friends, Ottoman and Rosalito, came by my crib. Asking about why I'm meeting up with a certain Miguel Evangelista."

"Fucking dicks."

"No – I'm the dick."

"And they're the assholes..."

They laughed, even if it was an old joke – or perhaps they laughed because it was an old joke. "Speaking of bugs, Rosalito planted one on my desk. These guys are so fucking obvious, though. Oh man – you wouldn't believe it: I actually saw the fuzz scoping out my spot while I was having a drink across the street. I followed them in. Truly amazing. Anyway, that bug is gone. As usual, keep talking like they're there."

Des and the Mechanic rolled up and joined them at the table.

The Mechanic started this round. "Nice scheduling with Newcomb, Bastard. I was in and out. Des did well, she's all right. The Organization's formula for the wave-delivery system for the White Dove is programmed within the NTC mainframe. I was successful in integrating our wave communications so that they ride on the others, but still ultimately and only target those receptors hit by the White Dove, and without disrupting those already being emitted by F-E 999 for its interests.

As we speak, we are already addicting the minds of the poor suckers who've subscribed to Rent Your Brain, and introducing dependency on our glorious White Dove." He drew on his cigar, put down the marker, and exhaled. "And I included our information – the address and phone number for Orange Vulture's warehouse – so they come to us and not to F-E 999. We'll be getting orders soon."

"Good job, two," Miguel said. "On my end: I spoke with Dr. Diemande earlier. He is finishing setting up Orange Vulture's receiving and shipping department – it's in a rented space in the east side downtown. So, just a couple blocks away. This place will be our base of operations. Here we will receive the shipments of the White Dove leaf. Leburik has instructed Diemande on how to process the leafs. Diemande will produce the powder extract in the laboratory and compose 5 and 10 milligram dosage tablets. We will soon begin producing 20, 30, 40, 60, 80, and 120 mg tabs as well, to keep up with growing demand and higher tolerance. These pills can be broken into powdered form and it's water-soluble. This way, we can allow our consumers to swallow, drink, smoke, blast, or bang the White Dove. We do want our customers to have a bit of fun with the pleasure of the ritual, no?"

M.E. had it all down. Bastard smiled. He raised his glass and so did all the rest. They cheered. "To the profitable future of Orange Vulture, Inc., and to the White Dove," he proposed.

"To our great fortune," someone added.

Everyone drank deeply, naturally (and some chemically) high.

"As the Mechanic was saying, the NTC wave virus is at this very moment newly polluting the minds of F-E 999's sucker guinea pig consumer-patient base, and at any moment we will begin receiving orders for our celestial product. I set up a new bank account today with Balls and Spoons Amalgamated, and we're all set for credit card orders, payments by check, photographs, brainwaves and VoiceBank deductions. The Accountant will ensure that no one is touching our balls, that all of our finances are in order. The Mechanic – your job is done, for now, at least. Sit back and collect – if you're needed again, we'll get in touch with you. Des – keep your job – if your boss doesn't fire or kill you. That's a joke – relax. Maybe not, I don't really the know the dude. On the serious tip, if you see this project through to a successful conclusion, you will officially become a member of the Organization."

Despi relaxed, then became elated, then attempted to suppress her excitement and maintain her cool. Miguel smiled, and continued, "Until then, know that you are protected as an honorary member. You have nothing to fear. You will not be killed. Maintain appearances. If you still have your job, do a good job.

"We will meet again tomorrow at the Loam. Most everyone involved in the White Dove operation will be present; you will meet the others working with us, and I will present the details of the following stages of our enterprise. Tomorrow morning, I will contact each of you to inform you of the location of the Loam as well as your specific (individual) time of arrival. Do not be late. Do not be early. Arrive exactly at your designated time. I'm sorry, Des, but this is explicitly directed at you, because you are new, although it of course applies to everyone here as well as everyone who will be in attendance tomorrow. Lastly, should you supply anyone or anything any information about anyone or anything regarding anyone or anything about this specific operation or the Organization in general, you will be summarily executed.

"Now, understand that each one of you will have to pass through a series of rigorous tests tomorrow before being admitted to the secret meeting room. Your appointments are staggered – hence, the emphasis on a punctual arrival. If you're late, everything will be pushed back, and Bastard and M.E. will be angry." Miguel read the eyes of his companions and was satisfied. Assured that his words had achieved the desired effect, he allowed his muscles to loosen, and he relaxed back in his chair.

"Finally, I'd like to add, truly, that I'm really excited about this new endeavor, and I feel honored and fortunate to be working with such a promising crew. I mean that – ask Bastard, I never say shit like this." Bastard nodded. "I have a good feeling about this." M.E. smiled. "Now, let's have a bit of fun...here's some White Dove for everyone. Let's get fucked up!"

The rest of the night I watched the four partners getting drunk and getting high, riding on the wave of their newly minted ocean of fermenting green balls.

Indeed, M.E. had done it again. Miguel Evangelista was, in the best sense, a brilliant producer. Over the years, he had established an amazing network of contacts and connections. There was no job that couldn't be accomplished by some member or affiliate of the Organization. All members of the Organization were anonymous to each other unless they had to meet for a specific job.

M.E. had his hands in everything. Two of each, if not more – that's his motto. From artists to lawyers, grocery store clerks to engineers, cab drivers to customs agents. Everything was free – there was nothing that any member of the Organization ever needed to pay for, so long as they followed the appropriate channels. It was a network founded on need, practicality, sustainability, and independence. M.E. was the nexus, the center of the wheel – from which the spokes of which extended to form a perfect circle. The pharmacist's toilet is broken? Fine, it's taken care of – because the plumber procured the priciest stones on the market from the jeweler, to give to his wife, and paid nothing for it – because the jeweler had had his teeth cleaned the week before – by the same dentist who needed some extra morphine from the pharmacist...and so on...

What goes around comes around. Institutionalized karma. M.E. had built an extended family structure in which everyone performed a specific function that was necessary and beneficial. In short, he was an anarchist, though terminological definitions seem too limiting, too human, for his particular social vision.

KISH DAY (FOUR)

19

RUMORS OF A GOOEY SKY.

And the next day we were summoned to the Loam, which I can speak of now only because it no longer exists, having been (deliberately?) destroyed during the Great Earthquake of 12002, which occurred shortly after our story here ends, which will happen later.

I arrived with Bastard at the entrance to the Loam, beneath the Grande Bridge. Having reached the base of the land connector, we climbed down from the road to the bank of the Dirty Water River. The entrance to the Loam was to be found somewhere here, on the shore, on the land between the lapping water riffles and the base of the Bridge.

Smartly situated, this moment's passage to the Loam. The Grande Bridge served purposes manifold: visually, to hide and shelter clandestine activity; auditorially, the constant 888888*** sounds of automobiles motoring and the noisy heavy industrial light hum the zooming zoom zoom, descended upon us low like a shroud like a radio blanket, and allowed us to speak freely to each other. After a few minutes searching, Bastard found the portal to the Loam. It was inconspicuously signed, X-marked by the symbol of a crab smoking a pipe, traced on the sand with a stick.

Getting into the Loam is a strange process, but you get used to it. Bastard entered into the earth, feet first, allowing his body to be thus embraced, engorged, engulfed, completely submerged, as he passed through a layer of land some four big lengths deep.

Having passed through the terrestrial flesh, he reached the top of an empty hollow within the earth, and subsequently fell through the air from the ceiling onto the floor. His landing was cushioned by a soft pillow of clam shells and porcupines; rising to his feet, kicking away some of the needles and abandoned calcium houses, he found himself in the middle of a large, cavernous, underground lair. Soon, he knew, everyone would be able to breathe and speak with ease.

The room resembled a waiting room of a doctor's office, except that where a glass window might separate the patients from the secretary and rooms in back instead stood a glass delicatessen case with meats and cheeses. A large mustachioed man behind the counter pushed out his lips, urging him to take a number. Bastard complied. When his number, 72, was called, Bastard ordered some cured meat and sharp pasteurized dairy product on a piece of floating baked grains – and immediately, Bastard materialized into a second room, without having physically moved a pubic hair.

This next space resembled a beer hall: high-ceilinged, spacious, with wood floors and long tables. Unlike that kind of place, however, within were approximately seven hundred and nineteen androgyns adjacent, lined up against the walls of dried mud. Each one held a long thick white candle, the flames of which cast manic, unpredictable shadows upon the ridged, uneven, tolerant wall and floors and ceilings. I wondered if it was more cost-effective to utilize these semi-beings than to go out and buy candlestick holders. Then I wondered who, if anyone, actually ran the Loam – like who was in charge of ordering more meats and cheeses and opaque androgynous nymphoids versus candlestick holders. But I was not allowed to entertain this line of thought for too long, for a carrot had sprouted up from the hard wet floor and was inviting Bastard to follow her through the following six of nine chambers that would lead us to our destination.

"Follow me through the following six of nine chambers that will lead you to your destination," is what she said. I looked over at Bastard, who pretended to ignore me. The carrot floated upward, and we followed suit, passing through the ceiling into the third chamber of the Loam.

"This is where your test begins," began the orange root vegetable.

"Why am I being tested?" gargled Bastard with alcohol. He swallowed.

She pulled out a notebook and flipped through its pages. "Oh yes, do forgive me, I didn't realize that you were the Minister of the Interior. I was supposed to have someone else at this time, but everything got rescheduled, you know, ha ha. Unfortunately though, now that we've started, you must go through with it – no way to turn back. Won't take long. Keep me company 'til my next appointment! ... Do forgive me."

"Forgiven. Let's just get on with it," Bastard sighed.

And with that we passed into the fourth room, so that I have no recollection of the third room to be able to relate its interior appearance to you with words. The fourth room was invisible, rendering visual description even more difficult. I recall a musty dank cool air, almost morning dew-like but foul rather than virgin; it got progressively thicker as we walked and walked, further and further, for what may have been twenty-four cinderblock kindling sticks.

The sound of struck flint opened a door into light. We had arrived within the foyer of the fifth room: a modest compartment that served as the mouth of a heavy maze constructed of ladybug intestines, soldered together to reach the length of the average of our three lunar orbits.

The carrot paused momentarily to allow us to change our shoes before leading us into the dark, damp, odorous tunnel. Trudging along the slippery rubbery floor, I felt a genuine gratitude towards the carrot for providing us with elephant-tusk spiked-sole boots. For, in less traction-impressive footwear we would have found our heads thrown to beneath our asses, horizontal upon the slick, slimy, sausage-skin street. After a few months, the cries of the ladybugs went unnoticed; and shortly thereafter, the light at the end of the tunnel drew us out.

We were hosed down with blue juice, scrubbed violently by rapidly rotating cylindrical brushes, and then blown-dry by enormous, beautiful cavities, before we could enter the sixth chamber. I was beginning to think that all of this was a bit much, but upon seeing the sixth room, I decided not to care.

Luckily, the shattering of the glass wall through which we crashed didn't cause any problems. A formally-attired man-person approached and seated us on opposite sides of an enormous bed that slept in the center of a lavishly decorated room, and we were invited to indulge in the most sumptuous of pornographic feasts.

Curtains of velvet drew back to expose a single

androgyn laying prone at the base of the mattress. Up at the headboard, some twenty voluptuous, naked deer-women cavorted excitedly, seemingly nearing the heights of climax – or perhaps perpetually dwelling there.

They groped each other madly yet sensuously; within some small circles, the nude, cavorting deer-women-things executed an awesomely choreographed dance of alternating cunnilingus and analingus.

The androgyn fed Bastard succulent grapes with super-extended arms outstretched until its previously unsexed midsection gave birth to an eight-stick erection that penetrated the air.

Somehow like that, Bastard and the androgyn came together, their semen joining in midair high above the lesbian deer, forming an intricate spider-web of seed that descended upon the frolicking fawns.

At the moment that I began lamenting the concealment of the deer-women beneath this thick sheet of sperm, I realized that I was sinking through the floor...

...And into the seventh room, of course, which boasted gold-encrusted velvet sheep who offered us their coats while we roasted marshmallows by their dry-ice-fishing hole; an entertaining entertainment troupe, complete with top hat, cane, and no underpants, entertained us; however, as the room stank of spoiled herring, Bastard decided to proceed directly.

I caught a glimpse of disappointment among the six or eight endangered seals as they watched us leave. Then they returned to the matter at hand – and rapidly flapped their fin-arms rabidly to escape the soaring spears of a hundred hungry hunters. We made our way away.

And into the most curious of all the chambers, being,

numerically at least, the eighth. This room existed in only two dimensions, having lost its depth in a card game (as was explained to us by the briefly absent but now again present carrot who subsequently disappeared).

It was some kind of glass plane. The next room lay directly ahead, and the previous one was visible behind. But how to proceed? One cannot walk straight through a room with no depth.

Physically unsure of myself, I waited for Bastard to make the first move. I could tell that he felt compressed, too.

But then, slowly, he began to move slightly upwards, seemingly inwards – it was perplexing, but he was moving through the room, and proportionately diminishing in size until he finally traversed the double-dimensional space and reached a door in the upper left of the glass. At that point, Bastard appeared to be one-seventh of his actual triangle.

I followed his example, and together successfully passed through the door and into the ninth chamber, where the two dear friends met again with great warmth.

20

VEGETABLE SOUP?

"I'm very glad you made it safely," M.E. smiled. He swept his arms and everyone sat down at a table in the center of the small room. The Mechanic and Des were already there, somehow – as were Dr. Diemande, Yusef Yusef Croniamantal, Sasia Stasia and NNannette Nonet. This surprised Bastard, who was supposed to arrive right after Miguel Evangelista and before everyone else.

There were eight altogether. Everyone was there – everyone in the Metropolisse chapter of the Organization that was directly in on the White Dove deal.

"I had no idea I was in danger. You mean passing through the nine chambers?" exhaled Bastard smoothly though tightly.

Miguel twitched a frame, as if barely sensing a fruit fly floating four fingers 'fore his eyes. "Oh shit – I'm terribly, terribly sorry, Bastard," getting up and collecting a bottle of whiskey and some empty glasses from the small bar against the wall. M.E. returned to the table and poured Bastard a tall glass.

"That's why you're late, I see."

"?"

"I have to dice that carrot up, peel it and slice it and dice it the fuck up. You like stews?"

"I'm afraid I don't quite follow you...but...I'm assuming you mean that – "

"She's a brat. A prankster. A mischievous, misanthropic miscreant who enjoys misbehaving by misleading my friends on mysterious and sometimes miserable missions. She was a mistake, and it was too late to get an abortion."

"So my grand voyage here..."

"Was unnecessary for you." M.E. shook his head, pissed off at the carrot. "After you pass through the mud ground ceiling at the Grande Bridge and land in that first room, you were supposed to go through the second door on the left." M.E. rose to his feet, crossed the room and pulled open a door, revealing the waiting-room cum delicatessen right fucking there. A small sign, tacked on the door, bore handwritten glyphs that spelled "Bastard and M.E. / Organization / Meeting Room / Enter Here."

"Motherfucker," rocked Bastard. "What a waste of fucking time."

"Again, sorry. But in no defense, it's an interesting trip, right? She's got a great imagination, and really good acid. I figure some of those chambers, you know, you might actually get your rocks off on some of her ideas."

"Yes, I did get to come, which was very nice. And all in all, it was an extraordinary experience. I'm sorry if I came across a bit punchy just then – I simply needed a drink. I feel much better now." He took a long draw on the grain. "But everyone's here – nice to see you all – so let's not waste any more time."

Bastard glanced around the table, everyone slightly nodding or otherwise exhibiting mutual pleasure. "So – what have you gone over so far?"

"Nothing much. We've mostly been sitting here in awkward silence awaiting your arrival. Everyone passed the test of the Loam, which is unsurprising, not least because everyone is here. I didn't want to proceed without you." To the others, "Everyone, though you may know him already by name, allow me to present to you the Minister of the Interior."

"Yeah, I actually know everyone here. Thanks, and thanks for waiting – but six months is a long time to wait. You should have begun."

"It hasn't been six months, my friend. Another one of her tricks. You're really only six ticks late. And I allowed for that potentiality. We've all only arrived shy-presently." M.E. grazed his eyes around the table, content.

"Oh wow, great," Bastard, glad he wasn't six months older. "So, everyone knows each other? Good. This is a housekeeping session. We will try to keep it brief; we can meet with any of you to answer any questions and delineate the details of duty. I trust that everyone received the telepathic dossier?"

No confusion.

Miguel picked up the thread. "So everyone is briefed on the job at hand and knows their places and their lines. Leburik obviously can't make it, though he is here in spirit and in brain. The basics, quickly: the Mechanic and Des know their positions. Dr. Diemande, as you know, you will be receiving and processing the White Dove leaf shipments – Leburik just sent us a shit ton more. Yusef Yusef – we need you at the warehouse.

You're in charge of Distribution – taking orders, shipping and handling and the like, street teams, and protection. As you will be working alongside the Doctor, you can also assist him with any science stuff.

"Sasia and NNannette – Bastard has been recently visited by Officers of the Nation Ottoman and Rosalito. He will undoubtedly be paid another visit; or, actively, they will undoubtedly visit Bastard again. We do not wish this attention to continue, much less escalate. Bastard has a lot of important work, and we can't afford to be fucked with on the regular. I'm counting on you two to devise a device or plan a plan to prevent this from repeating – we will gladly help you in the execution of this task. Upon minimal consideration, Bastard and M.E. figure the best way is for you two to assume their identities, their bodies, their beings, their minds, their clothes, their jobs. Cool?"

"Cool," they said together.

"Hey," the Mechanic interrupted. "Why am I here? I thought I was kinda done."

"Right, right. Very good question. I need you to collect a bunch of supplies for Bastard. I haven't even told you this, yet, bro," M.E. turned to Bastard. "Rumor has it that Lance Newcomb possesses a special secret stone or something that ensures his vitality. It's the reason for his longevity. He purportedly keeps this at his estate, in some crazy gallery of antiquities and oddities. The two of us will discuss this further at a later date. Anyway, for the time being, we need you," M.E. returned to the Mechanic, "to stockpile everything Bastard might need for a fairly extreme burglary."

"On it," he acknowledged.

Des had some reason for not speaking up. She still didn't know that Bastard and M.E. knew that Lance

Newcomb was her man. The two friends left enough space in the air for her to say something, but she didn't.

"Aight, so... We have our first major shipment arriving at second sundown. So far eighty-one thousand orders have been placed – all since last night. I want this shit turned around without a hitch, so we are all to begin carrying out orders immediately. Ladies Stasia and Nonet, I want Ottoman and Rosalito out of the picture sooner than later, or as soon as possible, whichever is sooner. Diemande and Yusef – please head straight to the lab. We have enough of the White Dove processed to handle this order, but we need you guys to start on the new batch as soon as it arrives tonight."

Miguel Evangelista coughed, pulled out some keys, and tossed them to Diemande and Croniamantal. Then he gave every else a copy, and said, "These are personalized keys, so we know who's coming in and out. No disrespect. Just business."

"Good. Des, for now, again – just keep your job. Report any bizarre, suspicious behavior to us immediately. Need you to keep F-E 999's business running as usual. Anything out of the ordinary may draw undesired attention upon yourself, upon Bastard and M.E., and upon the Organization.

"I will summon you when we need to meet again, which may not be necessary. Everyone knows how to contact everyone else, right? Good. If there is some crazy serious emergency, resort at once to telepathic communication with all. These are big stakes, friends, and the slightest mistake could devastake our dope schemescape. Like Bastard said, this meeting will be kept short. It is just about over now.

"In closing, I would just like to say, with a smile that only those with sight can see, that the Abbott has communicated (to M.E.) his sincerest excitement regarding our plan. If you don't know the Abbott, just know that he is important to Bastard and M.E.. We expect that everyone will do right by themselves and for each other and for the Organization. I don't want anyone going down for this.

"Finally, one last item – my Time in the Nation is limited; I will be returning back South in a few slips, as mandated. In my absence, work will continue. Bastard will be left in charge, he alone instead of us both.

"He will be in regular contact with M.E., but that is not your concern. You are to honor and obey and respect him alone, as if he were two."

"Word, I think we good here, then?" Bastard concluded. "Good," he decided. "I leave you with the wise words of the Genius: 'I got your back, but you best done watch your front.' Let's move."

21

FOUR DIVIDED BY ANOTHER NUMBER ALWAYS EQUALS _____ (FILL IN THE BLANK AS DESIRED).

I accompanied Bastard back to his apartment, where he prepared to get some real quality sleep for the first time since before the first page.

Upon entering his bedroom, he began his somnambular rituals. First, he removed all of his clothes, beginning with his shoelaces and buttons and zippers, which he placed in a small receptacle on a credenza. He then took off his shoes, pants, shirt, underwear, socks, undersocks, and nipple caps. He covered his genitals in a small silken sheath, walked over to a wooden dresser against the south wall, and pulled out a Continental Forest Tree Bread box, from which he pinched out a handful of pieces of cork of various sizes. These he lodged snugly into his each of his major cavities – his ears, his nostrils, his mouth, his anus.

Next, he proceeded to rub a thick gel upon his belly

with his forefinger in concentric circles around his navel. He repeated this motion an even seventeen times, with increasing vigor but perfect precision. From another dresser drawer he removed a thin, circular, mesh screen which he affixed to his stomach – held in place at its edge by the hardening adhesive gel.

From the large closet, he brought out a three-liter mortar and pestle, as well as a variety of unmentionable herbs and spices, which he ground into a coarse powder. Satisfied with its consistency, he spread out a sheet of adhesive wallpaper on the floor and dispersed the mixture — which I couldn't smell included cloves, nutmeg, orange peel, dead ants, hibiscus, black orchid pollen, granulated fish semen, rose hips, hummingbird bone marrow, chamomile, powdered cow blood, cracked dragon fruit skin, ground unicorn horn, crushed cucumber seed, sour cherry extract, leftover crack, and dried chili paste – evenly across it.

Having completed his bedtime preparations, he laid down upon the sticky sheaf, rolled himself up inside it like a blunt, and passed gently into the world of sleep.

KHAMSA DAY
(FIVE-0)

22

WHERE DID HE GO? (I WANT TO KNOW).

Which is, unfortunately, one place I cannot follow him. Which might be for the better, as I understand that Bastard's sleeping life is just as, if not more, wild and convoluted as his waking life.

Bastard has confided that he "capably engages" in a "fully formed conscious life with other people and places and things – philosophies, existences, moralities, behaviors..." and that his "dreamworld" is "... completely independent and different [ed. *of and to this life here now*]."

If I can figure out how to get in there, I expect it could be another book. Maybe more. Maybe less.

Might be for the better, I suggested, because having to understand and relate another simultaneously occurring and independent life of Bastard would push the land out furtherish. It would make this book at least another time again longer, too.

MOONDAY (SIX)

23

STANDING IN MOONDAY.

When he awoke, physically recharged, he felt warmer than usual. The heat of the suns shining through the window upon the sleepingFloor had fully melted the adhesive within the paper sleeping bag.

Bastard slipped out of the cocoon easily, removed the cavity plugs, and excused himself to wash in the toilet.

He did some shit in the bathroom, then reentered his sleeping room in order to walk to the door to his office – just in time to catch the end of his phone ringing. He heard the click of the answering machine.

Then he heard M.E. excitedly speak the words, "Yo! The fuck you at, B? Supposed to meet up yesterday. Haven't heard from you – what's up? Gotta talk, brother, it's actually important, for real for real for real for real. Hit M.E.."

Confusion splashed his face as he dried his hair with a real towel. Bastard stood in the doorway there, naked, as he realized that he'd just slept through all of yesterday. He was now standing in Moonday.

A SEPARATE HALF-CHAPTER.

"It's actually maybe for the better. That doesn't make sense. Anyway. You listen to the messages I left you?"

"Come on, Miguel," Bastard voiced into the mouth piece. "You know I would never do that." He wasn't dressed yet, and said, "I'm not dressed yet. Haven't even had a first dose of anything. I slept through Khamsa? That's fucking hilarious, brother. One of my least favorite days, anyway. But M.E., tell, what's going on?" Bastard then grunted as he bent over and pulled his sea blue water socks on and up his foot ankles.

"Not much. Two incredibly pressing and relevant issues, though. First, Lance Newcomb put out a hit on you. Through the Underworld Underground."

"Fuck, dude. He's connected with them, too?"

"Yeah man."

"Whatever. So how come I'm still alive?"

"Valid question. Took M.E. a minute to figure that out. How come you're still alive? Therein your question lies the answer to your question. You're alive, though you died. They wanna make sure they kill you right this Time, for forever."

"That's cool," Bastard observed. "Well, I hate to repeat myself, but, Whatever." He paused to consider the meaning of this before saying, "We make our own decisions." Then he said something else that I couldn't hear. Then he said, "Shit."

"Fair enough, Bastard. But now, you must go to Point West – today. Visit the Abbott. Straighten this out, protect your neck. Talk to the brother. See what he can do to help. And you know that cat will always help you – he fucking loves your dumb ass. He already knows you're coming."

"Shitfuck, this is fucking serious – and thanks, you're a good friend. It'll be good to see my brother the Abbott, but this whole shituation sounds really threatening. Whatever. Why the fuck do I keep saying that? I must be nervous. It's all good." Bastard clumsily clawed a cigarette out its cardboard casa and lit it before saying, "What was the other thing? You said there were two. Things. Two things."

"Today's Moonday."

"We established this already."

"Tomorrow is Wonderday, ass. The Official Conditional Beneficial Absolute Judicial Hearing starts to end tomorrow afternoon."

"Oh right. So what do you need?"

"Well, brother – you need to go West. You've a meeting with the Abbott tonight. He still has mad sway with the Underworld Underground. Did you know the Abbott was a Major Wizard back in the day?"

"Oh shit – I forgot that he used to fuck with them. Right on. Thank you."

"And what Bastard and M.E. need? Well, again, we need you alive. At least for another few days, and back here. Don't worry about anything else right now. You'll be back tomorrow in Time for the show. I have everything locked down until then." He took a one second break, then dinged, "Oh quick update since you were out: White Dove production continues and increases and continues to increase, increasingly, actually – and continually. This program thus far has been a huge success, Bastard. Yesterday's sales was bananas. Shit is going great. Once the trial ends, fuck knows what'll happen, and the Organization needs you here for that. And again, alive."

"Sure."

"Here's your ticket. You're on the first train Westbound to Point West after a series of many others, which all depart at specific Times before your train. Yours also departs at a specific Time, from Grand Middle Station. You leave soon. Take these balls," M.E. passed some bread. "Have a good trip."

"Fuck you. You know I won't. I hate that fucking place," Bastard smiled. "Anyway, good lookin' out, fam. I'll see you tomorrow. Oh and brother?"

"Yes, Bastard."

"Don't forget to wear your fall togs."

Hahaha, they laughed at the same time and hung up their respective phones at nearly the same time.

24

NO TITLE. (IT IS STILL USED AS AN ARMORY.).

The entrance to the Old Armory, which housed the newly rehabilitated Grand Middle Station, *showcased several sextravagant peripatetic phantasms perpetually in periphrasis, psi-creatures in glorified shields of bexium, alternately fixed plasmatic armoires bearing chests of amber gourds, beating the crests upon each armed guard's breast, and guarded arms folded against and across gilded chests of drawers, the rest left by the imperial army, the flowers of imperialist charms, as well as the harm of such foolish imperatives; when said mandates are asserted solely to draw forced conclusions from such importantly furnished intransigencies, they are foolheartedly expressed by the vacuum created by the vacuous drawing of empty lungs. Inflated by plain air, no less – something that no one could low nonger subsist upon, let anon resist a pawn – not for the least fur-coated reveries, revered for bloating rotted knots,* he thought as he ascended the stairs to the main hall.

When the shine of the phase of the fine face of the heroine of rebounded steel wool or bleed-wood technology ... you can't know when the noise knows, the body of the instrument speaks, re-noises, echoes. Chorus reverberates, remonstrates, then repatriates = then the expounded silence bears berths of pure fuel full energy. This is when the synergy of compounded astral efforts (what they revered most highly, in-fact-so=much even lower than that, was the hair that was shed from the heads of the toads, and which was subsequently, with no lack of irony, stored in stores inside the iron shed behind a curtain of vermilion veal stew) would run into lower depths and even slower roads, raining loads of locomotives and tracks and paths and racks....but it's the endelstein that really makes all the difference. Especially when plugged into the ministerio-transference abindino modulator (do not unplug the fQtM channel when performing this exercise in regurgitational suicide – for you may once come back ...)

Thinking the above, he approached the horizontal tier to await the train's arrival. He had thoroughly prepped himself for the trip, having procured (and then packed) a few phials of pharmaceuticals and a few flasks of flava. Bastard had to be plastered to accept train travel, to help him deal with having to deal with people; with big open spaces, with small enclosed places, with traveling, with having to sit next to people he didn't want to sit next to, which invariably happened, and so on. He had fortified himself over-abundantly, and his mind was having a gala dance.

"I don't want to go back out West," Bastard said to his brain. "I don't want to go at all. Possibly anywhere. But orders are orders; and it is important to follow orders when you have only yourself to give yourself orders and to take them from. If we are going to take down the

Ancient Imperial with the dust of the Dove, we must abide our own symmetrically laid out plans...

"Why the fuck did Lance Newcomb fatwah my ass," his mind meandered. "That semi-man's actions are consistently confused and confusing. He adopts a whole different line everyday. Motherfucker changes his mind more often than I fart."

"That's not possible," his brain replied.

Bastard regarded the largest Circhronometer in the Kingdom. It measured about thirty-five hundred decibels in diameter, and hung high up on the wall of the Great Hall of Grand Middle Station, about eight hundred long things above the Rose. He noted that he had a few Circles to kill before the specified departure Time of his specific Time Train's train.

So Bastard decided to explore the remodeled modern marvel of a marvelous train station, the newly re-famous Old Armory: Grand Middle Station, in the city of Metropolisse, (with)in the Kingdom's great Nation.

By the Time he'd made that decision, the appearance of the station interior had changed. Now it resembled a large warehouse factory – the really big factories, the ones that make warehouses.

The train platforms had become aisles, and the aisles were stacked with all sorts of things: trains, lumber, dried goods, really little things, boxes, coffins, freshly baked bread, garbage dumpsters, liquid ice, frozen food, cases of beer – even a small section of all-natural, organic industrial revolutions. Bastard stopped looking around when he logged that Aisle Fourteen was his platform.

He walked a bit in order to pick down a shopping cart from the hanging rack dangling from the centuries-tall, gloriously golden and nonsensically ornate ceiling. As you know, he had already decided to go exploring; now, he decided to buy some supplies for the trip while doing so.

"Let's go shopping!" said the voice from the hidden speakers that played opiatic drivel between Kingdom mandates and waterfalls, oceans crashing into waves, lava bubbling boiling.

He tried to ignore but obeyed. "Some fights aren't worth fighting," inside Bastard concluded. So he collected in his cart, for to buy, snacks for his journey. He grabbed some really tasty-looking molten parachute encrusted penguin's milk cheese (imported from Nearlandia, no less), some freshly baked Swaddle bread (aged four and a half Cycles), a pack of brand-new kangaroo shoulder blade spiced jerky, some bruises and negligibles, and so on.

As the space of the station expanded to include more and more things great and small, Bastard was able to get everything he needed – and more!

For example, he prepared to purchase extra artillery and ammunition by displacing these items from their original locations on shelves to a pallet with a fence around it that he pushed around. And he was thrilled to be able to afford all this shit with his cut of the earnings of the first fucking day of being in the White Dove business.

He grabbed more bullets for his NA Harpsichord triple-eight (that's three eights, or 3 8s, or 888), a knife sharpener (he'd forgotten his in the sink under the floor of his home), a brand new semi-automatic pea-shooter with ammunition included (for kids), a sturdy hardwire F2-automatic, which he'd always wanted – and which he was able to cop at a fifty percent discount because it was a used gun, not factory sealed.

He did look the piece over, first. It appeared to have barely been fired or even touched at all – it wore no scratches, scuffs, no residue on or inside the barrel. The action was sexy, and there were no obvious criminal fingerprints of doom. Everything seemed like new, and in great working order. And, of course, it came with the standard "Not-Even-Just-Once-Used-for-Killing-People Guarantee," which had to be stamped on every used gun's sales tag by an Official Inspector of Certified Produce, Handguns, Firearms, and Weapons of Minimal-to-Medium-Well Destruction, thereby making the sale of said piece not illegal.

With his new balls, he checked out with one of the millions of robotic cashiers. They all said "Thank you for your patronage" in unison whenever anyone paid for their goods and exited the line. Whilst performing this pronouncement solely for Bastard's patronage, his train began honking its horn to signal its own imminent departure.

"Clever large animal," Bastard said without a sound. It is unclear, but I believe he was referring to the train that knew it was leaving soon. He packed his legally acquired goods into his knapsack and walked some towards the train. As he stepped to its steps, it began, very slowly, to chug-chug-a-chug. This is the sound a train needs to make for to trigger forward motion along its track.

In a rush, Bastard climbed aboard Car Number Nine without deliberateness. When he figured out where he was, he recognized his mild great fortune. For all of the seats on the train were reserved, and he had accidentally crawled upon the exact car that held his seat – the one that he had rented for the duration of the trip.

He turned and walked down the inner-aisle towards his destiny.

25

IN WHICH BASTARD SITS IN A MOVING TRAIN IN ORDER TO GET OFF LATER.

He wasn't happy with having to take this trip in the first place, and it was already – immediately – becoming less appealing by the tick tock.

Bastard was not fond of public transportation and/ nor traveling. Not because he had anything against such or any kind of mode of transit, nor the act of physical motion, nor the experience of going to and being in different places. Simply because he did not appreciate forced proximity to strange beings.

He preferred to sit in a random seat of an empty row, which is uncommon because they are rare. But, and within reason, Bastard's constitution hoped for a seat with corresponding air and space and Time rights that were not compromised by an oversized foreign entity.

So when he saw a disgusting motherfucking shit-slab occupying the reserved seat next to his, Bastard was displeased.

Considering that he had just dropped most of his balls

on things to temporarily possess – only to face this calamity, Bastard quite cordially expressed some words through his clenched jaw. "I beg your pardon – is this seat taken?"

While dispassionately muttering those words, he pointed to the bodiless chair adjacent the late middle-aged, unconscionably overweight, man to whom he had directed the question. For a moment he thought that a funny expression – "middle-aged." But then he thought, "Whatever."

Again.

"Actually," sudden sneerking snivel sounds resounded, "contrary to appearances, this seat *is* taken."

Bastard hesitated before taking a closer look.

The man sweated profusely, as if perennially expressing a general disease and personal discomfort at the misfortune of having to exist. A flabby face was splotched with conglomerations of massive throbbing globules of perspiration and scattered shiny trembling pools of greasy oil that received and twinkled the artificial light from the fluorescent fixtures above.

His eyes gleamed beneath a shiny sheen of sticky slime that sheeted his sclera and sometimes binded his top eyelashes to his bottom eyelashes. Every time he blinked, he gave birth to an expanding web that would burst and splatter upon the inside of his glasses lenses as he re-opened his eyes wide. The tacky gold frame continually slid down his greasy nose bridge and magnified the viscous mucous that relentlessly purged from his tear ducts.

Snot leaked from a bulbous and pointy nose of two too-large nostrils that acted as upside-down volcanoes. A proliferation of shimmering orange-yellow wax funneled out of the loosely formed blob's ears, some of which accumulated on the shallow ridge above his earlobes. The excess flooded over the cartilage ledges to form the beginnings of what would undoubtedly become mountains of cloopy goop, founded on the shoulder pads of an unkempt, ash-gray sports jacket. His matching slacks were wrinkled and worn, and stained with a variety of indiscernible bodily fluids. His upper lip curled involuntarily, and some unknown muscle in his left eyebrow twitched rabidly. Bastard didn't need to get close to him to know that his breath reeked of sour egg foot vinegar.

But how could he accept that he could not sit in his seat? It was empty. The only signs of life – a trespassing newspaper and an encroaching overcoat – probably belonged to the unpleasant man with onion armpits with whom Bastard was now unpleasantly engaged. It could be someone else's shit, sure … but who and where was that someone else, and why and how could s/h/e/it lay claim to my shit?

Based on no further developments, Bastard grew increasingly convinced that those articles on his seat belonged to the sweaty onion man.

But the fat man's attitude was infuriating, and with everything else going on in Bastard's maniacal mind, he lost patience even before he was able to find it.

"Listen, motherfucker, you're being crazy fucking rude. I asked you a perfectly reasonable question, properly and civilly...had I known that this jacket and newspaper belonged to someone other than your obese ass...it was not an unreasonable or outlandish assumption, on my part, to think that they may have belonged to you. In my wild imagination, you could have easily picked them up and moved them to allow me to sit the fuck down... I would have saved my breath and never engaged you in the first place... For although I have no more interest in speaking with you now than

I had before you chose to cop a fucking attitude with me by replying to such a very simple, normal, and unobtrusive question – that I never would have voiced in the first place were it not necessitated by the absolute lack of any other open seats on this car – not to mention the fact that I paid for this seat, and that they are all reserved – see my ticket? – see the seat number here? – " Bastard flicked his ticket in front of the fat man's bulging eye bugles that were now popping out of his swelling head "– *and* that I'd asked in a respectful manner, apparently undeservedly – ... Man, I had absolutely no interest in interacting with you or any other dear asshole on this fucking train. I hope that whoever may await you at your destination will beat the shit out of you each and every time a sun rears its ugly head upon your sad, sad, head... – And if you contradict me, if you fucking talk back, I will have to beat the fucking shit out of you myself, right here, right now. I will derive great pleasure when I throw your sloppy ass off this moving train. And when I sit down... – and better yet, I won't have to talk to you anymore."

"The train isn't moving right now. We've stopped at the next station, just outside of town."

"Do you want to die?"

"Yes."

Bastard could see that this exchange was going to change nothing, and in an impressive instant of self-control, he walked away.

"What the fuck, though?" he thought to himself. "Why am I thinking to myself?" he asked. "Why is the train not moving again already?"

He looked out the window at the vast expanse of desert terrain that separated the habitable zones in the Nation.

The train *was* moving.

The fat man had lied.

26

BASTARD READS THE NEWS.
BASTARD ARRIVES IN POINT WEST.
ONLY GOING TO THE TOP OF THE HILL.
(DO SLIDING DOORS HAVE JAMBS [OR DOES
ONLY ONE]?)

During his criminal derelict junkie wanderlust phase (perhaps the wanderlust being the only phase he grew out of), Bastard had traveled quite a bit. He had appeared in most of the Unified Territories as well as a large portion of the Other Land(s). He had seen many lengths, he'd been many places, and he'd done many things over the course of his living life – much too much to recount here or even over there.

As he grew older, and most so while he was dead, Bastard traveled less. The Kingdom became more isolationist, making the Borderlands more inaccessible. In addition to synthetic changes and man's pimping of nature, the landscape was naturally constantly changing, making intra-Kingdom travel more and more difficult.

He still had friends and connections in random towns ... people he'd fallen out of touch with over the revolutions and cycles, perhaps, but people who would always get his back, black. Like the Abbott, a brilliant individual to whom Bastard would always remain blood. After all, this is the basic foundational fabric of the Organization's quilt, which is nice and warm.

When the train man came to collect tickets, Bastard was standing in the connector space link between Cars Nine and NineTen. He was staring out a faded window, watching the barren landscape blur together.

This part of the Kingdom was a uniform wasteland, and the high velocity of the train melted everything into an indistinguishable somethingscape.

Bastard exhibited his ticket and explained his shituation to the human worker man, who, ignoring his pleas to forget about the seating business and let him stand the rest of the ride until he reached destination Point West, left to have a word with the fat man.

When he returned, he reported to Bastard that there was no man there. Not only was he no longer sitting there, but there existed no record of any person having purchased a ticket for the seat next to Bastard's. He followed the worker man back down the aisle to discover that the fat man had, indeed, removed himself. He thanked the train man, and, after pretending to settle incomfortably for the remainder of the trip, began inspecting the immediate premises.

It didn't require much investigation to note the puddle of foul-smelling slop that the blob had deposited beneath his now absent butt, nor the traces of ear wax, mucous, snot, and shed hair that uglily graced the entire backside of the chair like an abstract expressionist canvas of doo-doo.

The newspaper and the jacket that had imposed upon Bastard were now hiding atop the soaked and stained seat next to him. The jacket smelled like a homeless man who'd soiled himself with his own shitty soil, and the newspaper smelled like it had been read by that same man.

Privately, he inspected the jacket, which to him felt like work. From the front right outside pocket, he removed a keychain with nine keys of various shapes and sizes. In the inside left breast pocket, he found several krillion balls and a business card that read Freeman-East Importing, 99 Worthington Street, No. 9 – aloud! every time he looked at it.

He moved the set of keys and the bunch of balls to into his pockets, and folded up the business card so that it would stop repeating itself.

The newspaper, *East to Point West Daily News*, was dated "Centerday, Franklin the 42nd, of the year KGGLMXIEleven." That was the day after the day after tomorrow.

In addition to the future day's date, the headline caught his attention: "Yesterday's Public Enemy Number One – Miguel Evangelista – Granted Extension of Stay in Kingdom of Nation – Temporary Pardon of Exile Endures During Duration of Guns and Butter Trial of Kingdom of Nation vs. Newt Humbert." He read on, but the article was vague, uninformative, misinformational, and poorly written.

Unable to stomach the stench that insisted upon putrefying next to him, Bastard got up and paced the length of the train. He reached one end and walked towards the other, keeping two eyes open for the fat man who had somehow vanished into impossibly thick air. Looking down at the graying blue carpet runner with fake plastic little light bulbs, he tracked a dotted line of dark green splotches that led him to the front end of the car.

This trace ended in front of a door on the north side of the train. The handle was dripping with thickness that must have dribbled down the fat man's arm, from his neck and his armpits, when he'd opened the train door.

But where did he get off? The train hadn't stopped since their conversation – it hadn't. The ticket checker was passing by and Bastard stopped him to ask, "Has the train stopped in the last fifteen ticks?"

"No, Sir, it has not. Although if you're wondering about the fat man, yes, he did get off the train."

"Where, do you remember?"

"No, sir – like I said, the train has not made any stops. This is a direct flight from Metropolisse to Point West. How is this confusing?"

Bastard pretended to understand the meaning of this, and decided that he could not, but did. He asked the conductor if he could be switched to another seat, complaining about the shabby condition of the seat and the foul odor that permeated the surrounding air.

"It's been taken care of. You may return to your seat, please? We do not encourage passengers to move around the cabin; and we require you to wear your body belts during High-Speed Speedy Gear Travel Time, which we will be entering momentarily. Please, return to your assigned seat, so that we may take notes, and study them."

"Of course," Bastard complied, and then complied. As he was buckling the body belt around his legs and waist and chest, he marveled at the cleaning job, which had eliminated any hint of the fat man's residue.

Shit – the jacket and the paper had been removed...doesn't matter...

And at that moment, the train entered into H-SSGTT,

and the motion of the train lulled Bastard to sleep the next few Circles...

The train pulled in at (;#)c.m..

The hotel wasn't far from Center Point West Station. Within a small circle, Bastard had successfully checked into and entered his room for the night.

He hadn't seen the Abbott in more than a few dead Circhronometers. In spite of the severe consequences of the immediate circumstances that necessitated their having to meet, it was a special occasion, and Bastard wished to dress fresh.

After performing some grooming rituals, Bastard changed into a brand new suit that Despi had sent him – a good voyage present. In a stroke of great fortune, she had had delivered his package via rail mail, so he was able to pick it up as soon as he got off the train.

Beneath the green mohair suit with matching pants and vest, he supported a rose-tinted oak brown shirt made of the finest snail skin, with silver buttons of charcoal lava chocolate larvae. All of the material was still alive, so his shirt and buttons moved ever-so-slightly like waves within themselves, as if breathing.

Bastard finished getting ready. He splashed kerosene on his face, and poured gasoline on his shoes, having left his aftershave next to the bottle of cologne in the kitchen trash under his bedroom. After applying blueberry gel to his soft brown hair and combing it through, he checked himself out in the full-length mirror on the door.

Satisfied, he headed out, locking the door to his room behind him, now in front of him, twenty-seven times for good luck. Not because he was superstitious, but because twenty-seven is what Time you get when you three times three three times.

And Bastard didn't want to be late.

Without hesitation, the rain commenced battering Bastard's blueberry gel-locked coiff' as soon as he stepped out onto the wet sod street. He'd forgotten his lid in the crib(!), but it was too late to turn back. His hair was already soaking blue.

Upon crossing the walk to the next block, he perceived a sensation of being followed. I looked around and, indeed, there was an enormously tall light-skinned man trailing our tails. He had very short legs and inconspicuous orange sheepskin sequined jumpsuit clothing. He maintained half a block distance the entire way to the Castle, shuffling his stumps hurriedly for each one Bastard stepped.

Up Balls-to-Hughes Ave., a left on Lumpy Street, and then a right, and straight up King Road, which was basically an alley that stretched up the mountainside of the first hill of Point West. [1]

Pavement turned to brick, brick to cobblestone, stone to rocks, pebbles to dirt and then into grass as Bastard reached the top of the mount where a huge flat steppe

1. The "first hill of Point West" was once known as "The First Mount of Point West." This is where Point West began its life as a future adult city. As it grew to become one of the top three most important of the seven major urban areas within the Kingdom, it grew westward.
When the Industrial Devolution imploded all major physical production industries and 3019's Atom's Disasters desiccated all of the land in the Nation, and everyone was forced to live in one of the three of the seven major cities*, Point West took on a near majority of the Kingdom's displaced populace. And still, the city expanded only west.
So the Castle on the hill, where the Abbott resides, overlooks the entire expanse of the cityscape as the eastern-most point of all the zips in Point West.
*No one was told which were the top three - those who chose to live in one of the other four of the seven major cities perished, along with those who stayed there because they lived there, during a subsequent census.

of beautiful lush green weed surrounded a driveway which surrounded a moat which encased another driveway that encircled the Castle – a giant skyscraper of a building, a cross between a medieval stronghold and a modern luxury condominium.

Bastard traversed the moat by canoe and the rest by his own two feet, using his hands only to open the gate to the entrance to the Castle. The sound of horse hooves and the proletariat chatting and fussing and hawking their wares played on the loudspeakers beneath the bushes that surrounded the steps leading up to the front door.

A large brass knocker made of hollow wood boomed a gong din when Bastard shattered it against the steel paper door. He entered a tiny vestibule. When the door slid shut on its tracks, the fourth wall was complete. A panel featuring buttons for a series of numbers begged Bastard to press the nine issue three times, and the little compartment became an elevator ascending up in Time.

27

SPACE IS THE PLACE.

DING!

As soon as Bastard exited the elevating room and entered the Abbott's living space, he forgot the outside. That the outside existed, that anything was out there – even though he had been there, for he had just come from somewhere out there, and it would probably resume when he returned to it. Entering the Abbott's was like crossing the threshold into another universe, another reality. Obviously, it was the same reality, just a different universe. But until then, nothing existed except this.

"All is intentional," the Abbott smiled in greeting.

"This is crazy," Bastard nutted. "There is nothing here!"

Indeed, there was nothing but space in the place. These things: light, air, open (non-) lines, openness. All was space, like there was nothing there. It looked like nothing; he saw nothing.

"Yup," the Abbott proudly accepted.

The High Lord's apartment/penthouse/entire floor/ condo level was indescribably glamorous (– it was a castle, though... Bastard knew this to be true, and not just because he had seen its exterior). Inside (- at least on the twenty-seventh floor -), everything was perfectly minimalist...but not obnoxiously so...so modern; cool – but not cold; ...tastefully austere, to the point that nothing was unnecessary. Nothing was necessary.

There were no doors, nor walls, for that matter...at least, none that wasn't invisible yet none that you couldn't walk through...they were just there for the appearance, as if they looked good, even though they didn't look. They were real walls and doors, though... they served the same function while being invisible, thereby maintaining a feeling of pure openness...

It wasn't until the Abbott gave Bastard the tour that I realized that indivisible and individual invisible panes extended from floor to ceiling around the entire level. Only the door to the apartment, which was also the door to the elevator, was not invisible. And yet, from the outside, the Abbott's residence had appeared as a normal stone structure in the style of a ninth millennium Auslandian countryside chateau.

"Nothing to see here," the Abbott joked. "Check this out – let's go to my office bar," he re-began. "You see: the glass is, quite simply, not simply glass. Nope! It is a new alloy that I've just recently come up with. It's more durable than anyone previously known to anything, and even more transparent than air!

"The other walls that you don't see – the interior walls, like this one we're coming up to right now," the Abbott appeared to open a door and directed Bastard how to walk next. "This is constructed of another material," his flicking wrist made a knocking sound. "I'm still working on its tensility – I hope to make this invisible material more sound. Make it structurable, for sustained stability. Those walls – that 'glass'" he pointed to something that preceded the outside, "*that* shit is strong enough to serve as the support structure for a building ten times taller."

Why this mattered, Bastard could not fathom. What was the difference – after all, who could know exactly what the walls were made of if one couldn't see them? Also, it sounded like he was just making the same thing again, in terms of final function.

Bastard was confused. He asked his friend if he had anything to drink.

"Of course, of course – that's why we're here, in my study!" the Abbott erupted with sincerity. He immediately proceeded to an invisible cabinet that was right before his face. When he moved his arm a certain way, Bastard could see a fully stocked bar. Three actually visible, apparently wooden, shelves supported three rows of booze bottles.

The Abbott poured out two glasses and four bottles, then grabbed four glasses and two bottles, which he pulled into a giant organ, carefully combining some of each of the six liquors in an ice shaker; this he stirred with a long, spoon-shaped piece of ice that proceeded to melt against the warmth of his cold, cold fingertips. He strained the concoction into the cocktail glasses.

During this process, the Abbott relayed, "When I first had these new walls and furniture installed, I had post-it notes stuck to each and every piece of furniture. 'Bar,' for example, or 'Bed Sheets,' or 'Beach,' or 'Bathroom Towels,' or 'Bidet,' 'Bleach' or 'Bananas' – everything in here that you can't see. Otherwise, I couldn't find anything at all! After a few Circles, though, I got used to it. Now I have the entire space and everything within it pre-memorized in my re-memory."

He pulled a pad of sticky papers from his back pants pocket, which was actually a sewed-on kangaroo pouch, wrote "S(h)it Here" on it with the squid ink pen that he kept in the right breast pocket of his purple tuxedo shirt, and placed it a couple of feet above the floor, where it appeared to hover.

"We are now in my study," he refrained, moving around what I fairly assumed to be an invisible desk; he sat down on an invisible plane behind it. "Do sit down, Bastard, and mind the parenthetical 'h' – I'm running low on post-it notes, and it can get ugly when one of my guests can't properly locate the shit-station. It's a matter of conservation."

"Do you entertain a lot still, then?" Bastard asked.

"No, not at all."

Bastard felt around with his hands, making out the contours of what sensed like a chair, until he was comfortable enough to sit down on something he could not see. He made himself as comfortable as he could, with the aid of the majority of the drink – which, thankfully, he could see. He sighed and glanced around the room, seeing nearly nothing.

"When I was looking at your place, coming up, the whole facade looked like a castle. How -"

"Oh ha! Yes. Pretty amazing, right?"

"?"

"It's paint."

"?"

"A new kind of paint!!! You can paint anything with this shit. And you can see through it if you're on the other side."

"?"

"You see that elevator right there, yeah?"

Bastard nodded.

"That's 'cause it's painted. Same shit. But that's

painted on both sides. The exterior walls here are only painted on the outside, so you can see through them, it looks like nothing is there, when you're standing in here. This is my ultimate defense: when the next Final War begins, if the enemies ever reach the base of my mountain here, I will dump all this paint thinner," the Abbott pointed straight up, "and the Castle will disappear!"

"I was gonna ask about that water tower – "

"Yup! Full of paint thinner. So I just pull that bit of string, tipple topple ipple-ito and bong – I am gone!"

"Except you yourself, my friend, will still be visible, right?"

"Yes! And how much crazier is that? Anyone looking at the place will see that I'm floating twenty-seven floors high."

"Dude, all of this is pretty fucking awesome and totally fascinating, but I gotta talk to you about some shit of immediate importance."

BASTARD AND THE ABBOTT TALK ABOUT SOME IMMEDIATELY IMPORTANT SHIT.

"Yeah," the Abbott acknowledged his pre-knowledge. "I know you know that I spoke with Miguel Evangelista already. That's why you're here, brother. M.E. said that Lance Newcomb done auctioned your name, Bastard, as an expensive bullseye. And the Underworld Underground has sights on you?"

"That's why I'm here, my brother," Bastard began...

BASTARD GETS WALLOPED AGAIN.

It was still raining when Bastard left the Castle and began his descent down the mountain and into the dark city night.

Bastard felt good: he'd had a swell time catching up with the Abbott, and he knew that his friend would come through. The Abbott had ensured him that he had the Underworld Underground cool. But that was the only thing the Abbott could guarantee.

Words seemed to carry little weight in this world. But Bastard felt good, knowing that some of the Abbott's words were heavy solids.

Distastefully, the tall man with short legs reappeared out of the shadows and pursued his pursuit. He followed Bastard most of the way back, only disappearing as soon as we reached the block upon which the hotel was originally built, and where it still stands to this day, further down the way.

Walking the hotel corridor, Bastard's nose hairs

pricked up a repugnant odor emanating from...what turned out to be his room. The door was open a bit... he pushed it as quietly as possible, held his breath and prepared himself for the worst – but the unit appeared completely empty. Whoever had been there...looking for what, though?... had already left.

All that remained was a cloud of stank that hung in the air, raining odoriferous gel capsules that, when popped on contact, defecated pebbles of green-brown-yellow-gray-orange mucous, sweat, piss, and shit. He thought about the fat man on the train...and couldn't get the notion out of his head that he knew who that man was...it hadn't occurred to him at first, on the train, but yes – of course – he should have known...that was The...

But he didn't have much time to work out this complexion – for at that instant, the minions of darkness came over the walls and overcame him, and Bastard was helpless but to retreat within:

"I can see people to my left and right, just barely within my peripheral vision, shadows lunging and lurching and leaping and lingering about, the darkness of the shadows of the shadow of the edge of my vision's scape, which is only a shadow of my mind and the sides of my eyes of the darkness of the bounds of the edge of my brows and it's mine, yes, it is mine, you see, or a sea of mines, lines, landscape of eyebrows and time, yes, boroughs with boundaries of signs of hedges and bushes and names of lines and lines and lines, delineating the darkness of the shadow of the shadow of my mind, the eyes of the sighs of the edges of the sides that surround my eyes (really just my visionscape). And all of these lines are chaos and everything and everyone is jumping around the room and some of them are crashing into me and pummeling me and as the pain within me, upon me, increases, my sense of self

141

diminishes into the lines like the lightning that pierces my mind, scraping shards of shadows of sharp light until I can no longer feel the barrage of fists and boots and my body, for a split second, becomes numb; the dark clouds close in, the black ring circling and circling, encircling my brain, until there remains nothing left to close in on...nothing left to feel but pain, the pain that becomes numbness, until nothing...

And I am an amorphous blob, sinking into the carpet on the floor, melting into a puddle of flesh...or, melting, I become a puddle of flesh...not saying that there was a puddle of flesh that I was melting into...I melted into, meaning became, eventually, a puddle of flesh...that is how I felt...could barely feel..."

When the minions of darkness dispersed, they left Bastard's body prone and bloody, bruised and broken, in a pool of his own, ideally dead.

30

RESET: SOMETIMES HAVE TO.

When Bastard woke up, circles later, it took him a few circumferences to locate his arms and legs.

He felt like a bundle of sticks haphazardly thrown into a dark black body bag. Summoning some remnants of energy and will, he managed to pull himself together and push himself up off the ground.

For a moment he considered returning to the floor. It looked good from where he was standing. He felt like going back down there.

He managed to convince his legs to do their fucking job and keep him standing up right. He then made further demands and persuaded his legs to walk his ass over to what looked like a very comfortable couch. He needed to sit down, get his bearings, figure out what to do next.

Luckily, it was a couch. And it was comfortable. Very comfortable. He exhaled deeply, though he could not remember having inhaled.

Cushions.

They took Bastard by the hands and led him down the road, where unconsciousness had laid out some wondrous, clean, soft, new sheepskin silk sheets...

WONDERDAY (SEVEN)

31

THE FIVE CORNERS OF A SQUARE.

What the fuck was that all about? I didn't think it would happen so soon – and right after visiting with the Abbott... And why didn't they actually kill me, instead of leaving me half-dead and half-alive.

"This place isn't safe," Bastard said quietly, to himself, aloud. "I gotta pack up my shit and get out of here as soon as possible." He made a wire-line and purchased a seat on the next train heading East, then packed up his things.

Bastard knew how to get to the East Point West Central East Station of Point West from the hotel; he grabbed his shit and made moves. He considered cabbing it to the train station, but figured he had enough time to take public transit, and thought perhaps it'd be easier to lose a tail underground, if he needed to.

He approached the entrance to the subway, grabbed hold of the green painted iron handrail, swung himself over and began descending: two or three steps, only – before he realized that he was going down to the wrong platform. "Downtown Only" read the sign above, and he needed an uptown train to take him to where There was.

Bastard looked around: he was on the northwest corner of X Street and 22nd Avenue; since he wanted to go uptown, he needed to find an entrance on the east side of 22nd Avenue. He thought that was where he had been – on the east side...but he didn't think about it long enough. Each of the four corners of the intersection had a subway entrance; the two on the east side for the uptown tracks; the two on the west side for the downtown-bound trains...

Perfunctorily, Bastard crossed the street to the northeast corner; but when he reached the curb, he noticed some wooden boards surrounding the entrance to the stairs. He hadn't noticed them before... A few more steps revealed that the wooden boards blocked an otherwise usable staircase down to the uptown train. Confused, he didn't think thrice, and bounded south to the other entrance for the uptown train, on the southeast corner of the intersection. Hopping onto the sidewalk from the street, he took three or four long strides towards the subway entrance before his mind registered what his eyes saw: orange construction fence-tape blocking the entrance, taped to the left and right green iron handrails, upon which the words "Caution – Keep Out – Danger" were illustrated by letters.

"What the fuck?" Bastard looked around again at each of the four corners of the street. Both of the entrances on the east side of the avenue were blocked – boarded up with wooden planks and/or surrounded by orange-plastic-tape-fence. No way to catch an uptown train here.

Confusing...very strange. He figured he ought to cross the street, to the southwest corner, and try the entrance for the downtown subway; he could take the train one stop in the wrong direction and transfer underground for the uptown train – and he knew that at the subsequent station south (which was too far away to walk to at this point), one could do so.

After impatiently waiting at the street corner for several moments to several hours – frustrated seconds baked into irretrievable minutes of wasted life only exacerbate the value one places on Time – the "DON'T WALK" sign changed (it changed to "WALK," if you absolutely must know), and Bastard was able to cross the street.

And so he crossed it, one step at a time, as most people not only cross streets, but walk in general. He stepped up on the sidewalk and, nearing the subway entrance, he reached out for the iron railing that would normally descend, along with the stairs, to the platform.

But, as he jumped down in preparation to propel himself along down the stairs, his body jerked back and awkwardly upright and to the side, convulsing inappropriately and unnaturally as his feet landed on hard flat cement. The pain that shot through his back, from his legs up to his shoulders and neck, accompanied his eyes' acknowledgement that there existed no stairs to descend. Just concrete, level with the sidewalk, as if someone had simply constructed a false subway entrance on a random corner of the street, or as if someone had just filled the pre-existing station full of concrete – either way, all the more perplexing because whatever had happened had occurred in the split second between the moment he'd jumped down and the moment he landed, unexpectedly, on level ground.

His body had been ready to leap down eighteen to thirty-two stairs, three or four steps at a time, and it had gained a decent amount of latent momentum – fattened by anxiety, expectancy, and false starts. Crashing down upon the concrete sidewalk, he crushed his legs, his spine, his bones, his muscles, and everything else he could feel in his entire body, into a space that was painfully smaller than that which it was intended to occupy in order to exist naturally and comfortably. His lower half felt as if someone had compacted it in a vise. The center of his back...crackling and splintering his feebly fumbling bones...

This spontaneous, violent compression left him with a swollen knee and a newfound lust for life.

He pushed himself up on his hands and knees, starting with his forearms and thighs, and lifted his head just enough to check out the northwest corner, where he had initially begun this peculiar psychedelic Sisyphean pyschsersize. But there was no kind of anything there anymore. No subway entrance – it had disappeared, straight vanished.

He crossed back up north towards the bare sidewalk corner, bemused, amused, confused, demused, and femused – not to say gemused. He had to see it up close. He knew that there had been an entrance there...

Indeed, no trace remained.

Bastard got up and scanned the other two corners. His stomach sank like lead in a lead balloon that was also sinking. He had already known, but it still hit him hard: there were no subway entrances on any of the four corners.

No sign of their existence.

What is happening? Bastard tried to think. Some force was preventing him from leaving this city, and/or from returning home.

"I have to get out of here..." Bastard kept trying to think. "...I'm not safe here...something really bad is going to happen, and I'm afraid it's gonna happen very soon. Fuck."

Then he saw two female sambar (no mobile penis) crossing the street – but then they were dogs, with heads of sheep. Perhaps the other way around.

One had a shaved head; the other's head had crazy balded.

He remembered so I told her you never gave M.E. the nineteen dills I won from you last night when you were teaching me how to play cards and I was flying over the tops of the chain link fence.

Despi smiled as she waited – she had just appeared before him. Looking at him, she pointed to a fifth corner. It must have just come into being, for Bastard knew that it had not been there before. Not only did he distinctly remember the four distinct corners of the intersection, but also he couldn't explain the mathematical possibility of the physical existence of a fifth corner at an intersection of two perpendicular streets with four corners. But on that fifth corner, now, was a subway entrance. He reached over to grab Despi'kha's hand, figuring they'd walk over there together. But there was nothing to touch, and his fingers passed through hers.

The image of Despi dissolved into the ether, which Bastard subsequently huffed, never one to waste.

Completely loopy, concentrating way too much on bending a knee each time he lifted a leg and placed it forward...one at a time – first one, then the other – he approached the newly materialized subway entrance. He felt like he was growing significantly taller and taller with each step, although he really wasn't growing that much.

But the green painted iron handrails of the subterranean entrance were getting bigger and bigger –

until they had enlarged enough to be equipped entirely, eternally, excitedly, en masse, avec enticingly encroaching entrepreneurs. Yes, as you probably guessed – it was then that the handrails morphed into a giant praying mantis, its antennae twitching about, a full twelve flowers from the ground.

The enormous insect, writhing in stasis, reached out its skeletal pincers and grabbed the big Bastard – not forcefully, but not gently, either –, picked him up, and carried him toward its stomach. As he neared the crackly grass-colored exoskeleton of the monumental Mantidae, a hole appeared in its center and opened wide.

Through this, Bastard was swallowed into the darkest of depths.

32

COWS HAVE FOUR STOMACHS.

When he regained consciousness, he barely observed that he was in a dark, dank cave...some kind of underground lair, again, and he breathed in the air.

A dim glow about twenty feet in front of him struggled through cracks around a door, illuminating the shape of its frame, which was the shape of a door...

Bastard planted his feet and trod upon the natural aluminum-glass earthen floor towards the light. He felt until he found a handle; he pressed down upon it, pushed the door open, and stepped into a small foyer.

It was an unassuming preface to the beautiful and bizarre subterranean space that followed: an enormous underground cavernous hyperbolic paraboloid with four main chambers. Each of the chambers would feature a unique infinite circuit of sonic vibrations that, although perpetual, became audible only upon physical presence. Once heard, each room's sounds persisted, until all four instruments were heard in unison, performing together.

Bastard would have to find his way through the four

hearts to hear the song. Then – then, he knew, the boat will come.

In the first chamber, the floor of which was barely visibly covered in white sand: a cello, plucking harmoniously, matched the amplified staccato of cricket legs scraping and tiny larvae bustling in large groups in small spaces. The combination of sounds generated was equally peaceful and disconcerting, soothing and unsettling, like getting a massage while spiders crawl over your body. Bastard shuddered, inhaled deeply the asbestos air, walked by the focused cellist, and crossed the room toward a logical sausage.

Through which he transported himself into a second chamber. The brightest lit of the four rooms (which he did not yet know but noted later), it was very gray and very cold. In the center of the room, a viola parlayed with the screams of the Seven Furies and a choir of humans moaning at a beloved's funeral. The sounds of the first room continued on in this second room. We passed by a burial ceremony, with mourners dressed in hooded black dresses, three times, before he located the door to the third stomach.

This one resembled a battlefield in sight and smell and taste. Alongside strewn bombshells and atmosphere-per(in)vasive chemicals and smoke and gas, the sound of a violin mimicked the piercing glissandi of wailing ambulance sirens and air raid warnings. The three rooms were now playing together: a trio of cello, viola, and violin, with the sounds of insects and Furies and mourners and explosions and sirens.

Dodging bullets and bombs and the bayonets of a charging brigade of ebullient Boy Scouts, Bastard successfully reached the far end of the room and safely passed into the fourth chamber. Adding to all of the previous rooms' accumulated sounds, the fourth room contributed a contrabass and an argument being held between four disagreeing elements: air, sand, water, and fire – whistling, dusting, boiling, bristling.

The aggregated sound of the four rooms, with each sonic element co-existing simultaneously, generated an amalgamated symphony of hell that was both painful and numbing to Bastard's ears.

The chamber music continued as Bastard entered the exit artery – a long, dark tunnel that contributed its own musical supplement. From somewhere above in the eternal darkness emanated the ethereal, tinny tremble of wind chimes, while from deep below shuddered aggressive, threatening rumblings of shifting tectonic plates, heaving earth, gas fast against mass.

The planet hiccoughed deeply, chuckled to itself, and then farted, excreting Bastard with its passage into an egress comprising seventeen flights of creaking, twitching, breathing stairs.

Turtledove air machines swamped with lost troubadours like bats high on hyena blood blocked Bastard's beguiling climb up, up and up, up and up. Smooth plastic tubes encircled caterpillar wombs like cocoons of faux-silk doom, hanging from the bottom of the beautifully base ceiling above him, some of which dangled so low as to nearly reach the tops of each step, furthering the challenge of Bastard's ascent.

Upon finally conquering the last flight of stairs, he found himself on a small landing. Looking above, he observed a circular panel marked "Emergency Exit Only – Alarm Will Sound." A ladder of nine rungs led to the manhole-like portal. Without hesitation, he climbed up the ladder, turned the handle, pushed open the lid, and . forced himself out – into the open air, at last.

He was now standing on a wooden pier, the iron

manhole cover having transformed into a flowering vagina of crepuscular predators. Since it was no longer dusk, the carnivorous vespertines remained docile.

Bastard traversed the pier to its end and waited in silence. The only sounds came from the black ink water ripples that slowly splashed against the dark wood pillars that supported the ligneous landing.

Then the hum zoom of a motor, at first barely perceptible, grew louder and louder. We sipped our beers in the bare luminescence of the stars above, the stars that lay beneath the land, embedded in the terrestrial crust. Their shifty reflections scattered across the soft surface of the sea.

Bastard coughed. The boat slowly cohered from the darkness. The engine stuttered and coughed off as the dinghy cut through the peaks of the remaining gentle dark waves. Bastard caught the rope that was tossed to him. He pulled the vessel close and hopped into the skiff.

"Where to?"

"Back East."

The engine kicked up again; the boat turned around, and we headed towards the horizon's birthplace.

33

BACK EAST.

Bastard's eyes opened to see a dock approaching. Then he remembered that he was on a boat, and it was more likely that the boat was approaching the dock.

"Where the fuck are we, helpful boatman?"

The image of the strange seafarer neither moved nor spoke.

Looking up through the dark, Bastard regarded the second moon. It floated within the blackness above, motionless and silent. Just like the boatman, Bastard noted.

Oppositionally, the first moon seemed to hurry, as if delighted to be setting. Together they offered enough light for Bastard to see Despi standing at the end of the wooden pier, waiting. She winked at him, but he didn't see it, which rendered her act disheartening for one rather than heartening for two.

She caught the rope and helped Bastard out of the vessel. But instead of securing the line, she threw the rope back. He turned around to see nobody catch it. There was no man, and there was no boat.

"Here," Des wrapped a dry blanket around him. Only then did Bastard realize that he was all wet.

"Thanks, baby."

Using the towel with purpose, he took advantage of the Time to appreciate her physical appearance. He admired her face. It featured a smooth forehead. Nice eyebrows. A pair of regular eyelashes bookended two cat-green-gray eyes. She had a nose, and both nostrils were neither curiously tiny nor unnervingly craterous. Graceful, intelligent lips. At the bottommost tip of her face, a reasonable chin.

The long, autumnal blond hair that grew from the top of her head splayed down over those shoulders that were still so neatly formed. Her body's sweat-tears, inspired by the thick heat of a dense night, flittingly caught shards of moonlight and accented her soft skin.

The wings of the bird in Bastard's chest that operated his heart fluttered excitedly. That body of hers, that he wanted. Her perfect curves, her beautifully shaped breasts and ribs and torso and hips and ass and legs and ankles. Shapely and irresistible, so nice, he wanted to touch her, he wanted to feel her, he wanted to love her again and again and again.

He thought about her naked, and about them both being naked at the same Time together.

Also, her dress was nice.

A light breeze interrupted his musings by introducing a sense of her perfume. He inhaled through his nose as their lips met about a passionate promise of pending consummation of savage desire.

"How did you know? That I'd be here? Now?"

Des looked down at her shoes, and so Bastard looked

at them, too. They looked uncomfortable. Her shoes. To Bastard.

They returned their eyes to eye level.

"When you hadn't returned from Point West City on schedule, Miguel telephoned the Abbott, who explained everything. Newcomb isn't fucking around anymore, it seems – but we know the old saying, about how seems can appear different. He had you followed from your hotel to the Abbott's and back; The sloth sicced the minions on you, and then – "

"Yeh, believe it or not, I'm aware of this. Wasn't sure it was all Newcomb, but kind of assumed since most of my enemies are dead. I was afraid that the fat man on the train was The sloth...which you've just confirmed, thanks...and of course, I knew I had a tail while I was out West. But see – those were non-violent aggressions. Part of the game. Intimidation tactics, or so I presumed. Fucking hell, babe. I didn't think this war would start so soon. I guess no one ever does. But the Abbott was supposed to buy me Time. That's why I fucking went out there! I wanted life insurance, not a death certificate. But I understand...even the Abbott has his limitations."

"Instead of securing your safety, he confirmed your location. As soon as he realized what was happening with the subway entrances, he immediately sent Charlie to bail you out. Without the Abbott's help, you'd be dead – for real this Time."

"You mean the impossible fifth corner???"

"Come on, Bastard. You know that two perpendicular intersecting streets produce only four corners!"

"Yes, I know that. And the praying mantis?"

"Again – a fifth corner cannot exist where there can be only four. Therefore, there was no fifth subway entrance. You think a giant praying mantis can simply materialize out of an iron handrail? Just cause it's green? That's racist. Anyway, that was Charlie. One of the Abbott's closest allies. A true soldier."

"The praying mantis?"

"Yeah. And you have the Abbott to thank for Charlie's help. They saved your ass. And thank all the asses in the world that they did, because I love your ass. Absolutely irresistible." She kissed him again. "While Newcomb was deleting those subway entrances, The sloth was on his way to smother you. Hence the deliberate pacing of the erasing of the stations. One at a Time, slowly. To confuse you, to literally give you pause. To give The sloth enough Time to get to you. That slow, fat fuck. Another few small circles and you would've been – "

"I get it," Bastard processed, although he did not understand why Despi'kha had said the line, "That slow, fat fuck." He found it odd, and commenced thoughtfully pursuing its possible meanings. He responded, "I'll be sure to send the Abbott a symbol of my deepest gratitude, and include one of equal or greater value for Charlie."

Bastard hadn't realized how long the decrepit pier extended. They had been walking for a while, he thought – and he knew they were still walking. But he was tired, which exacerbated his already deficient spatial perception, so he couldn't be sure.

He coughed, pulling a corner of the no longer dry towel up to his face. "Thank you for the towel, baby." He covered his mouth with it and coughed again. "How did you know I would need it? I don't remember being wet – in fact, I don't think – nah, I know – I was completely dry until I got out the boat."

"I can't explain that. The science of the Underground River. It's not complicated though, not at all, really. If you think about it for half-a-cunt-hair's of a small circle, you'll comprehend. Think about it, Bastard."

"I understand, thanks. Makes sense." Bastard respected the requisite possibilities for the existence of the Underground River, and the reality of its actuality.

Despi continued. "The Underground River is an Ancient Secret...doesn't matter. I mean, it's not to be known, let alone utilized. The Abbott took a big risk getting you out that way. You know he used to run the Underground Underwater of the Underworld – you're lucky he's a friend of yours. No one outside the Immediate Family knows about it. You're the first."

"Don't use the word Family when you talk about the Order. Please. The Organization is a Family. The Order thrives on oppression. There is no love. The Organization thrives on mutual support; on love and respect. That's Family. Don't confuse the two – seriously. Makes no sense."

"Whatever. Point is, you're here, Bastard; safe. And look – we're almost home."

She was right – they were already on the block. Before they turned the corner onto his street, before his view up the avenue was obstructed by large brutish buildings, Bastard looked back.

Everything was where it was supposed to be, and he felt relief.

He was in his neighborhood.

Then he was in his home.

He'd made it Back East.

34

NO ONE EVER TOLD THE UNICORNS THAT
THEY ARE EXTINCT, WHICH IS WHY THEY
STILL EXIST.

That night, Des filled Bastard in about what had happened during his absence, while Bastard filled her up with his semen.

Between sessions, they continued an accompanying intercourse, wherein she informed Bastard that M.E.'s trial was proceeding smoothly, and that M.E. had been granted an extension.

Bastard recalled having seen today's newspaper headline. Yesterday, on the train. He told her. He asked, "Was the headline *Public Enemy Number One – Miguel Evangelista – Granted Extension of Physical Presence Privilege in Kingdom of Nation – Trial of Nation vs. Newt Humbert Continues*?"

"Yup," she confirmed, "something like that. Anyway, the High Court decided, late last night, that the case against Newt Humbert required more Time...now they're saying that they need some kind of proof...more information on Newt Humbert – who the fuck he is, where the fuck he came from, where the fuck he is. Hilarious that only now they finally wanna know who they're prosecuting. Who the fuck M.E. is testifying against. So they made certain demands.

"Miguel of course agreed to help – he even told them that it was his 'civic duty' to comply. At which point one of the judges reminded him that he had been Exiled, and therefore he was not a citizen of the Nation – inferring that the notion of civic duty was inapplicable, or else misapplied. To which M.E. replied, 'You can take M.E. out of the Nation, but you can't take M.E. anywhere else!'

"He realized that he'd completely fucked up some words and lost meaning, but he was able to keep it together. 'That didn't work,' he dismissed. 'Strike that failed sentence from the record! Point is, I am here in this city, right now, and this city will always be my Motherisland. So this is a task I must perform.'"

"HA!" Bastard snorted. "Motherfucker is funny as fuck. Love that dude. How is M.E.?"

"Ech...he says he's doing fine. But he's being kept under close scrutiny by the Official Officers of Order for the Obvious Good of the People (OOOOFTOGOTP) – "

"Fuck."

" – for his own protection, as they say, until they locate Newt Humbert, supposedly."

It felt good to lay in his own bed. Bastard was exhausted, but his mind was still on. He listened to her voice, he listened to her words.

"Miguel asked me to oversee the operation until your return. Everything is good." She exhaled vestigial excitement. "I'm glad you're back."

The more questions he asked, the less he understood. The same shit was the same: Doctor Diemande and

Yusef Croniamantal continued production of the White Dove. Sasia and NNannette ensured everyone's safety and now assisted with distribution, too. All was going well. The Organization was making bank – mad balls. Shit was burgeoning. Demand for their drug continued to increase. But it all meant nothing, ultimately.

Bastard didn't like what she was saying. He was sleepy. He wanted to ask her how she'd been entrusted to run their whole operation while M.E. was locked up and he was out of town. But he couldn't form a proper sentence, and instead tried to not want to know. He probably did ask her, though. Can't remember. Bastard was losing focus. His other world was demanding his presence.

Is this all part of M.E.'s plan? Does M.E. really trust her enough to leave her in control of the Organization's White Dove Operation? And if M.E. does trust her – why?

Also, why doesn't Des level about being the wife of Lance Newcomb? That's a pretty big deal, and relevant.

Bastard felt comfortable and warm in his bed, even though he didn't fully trust the woman next to him. His mind drifted slowly, kind of like driftwood, but not really. Her body was warm. His was warmer. Between the mattress and the bed sheets, Bastard felt snug, secure and loose, like a piece of meat cushioned in a thick sauce, embraced by bright green leaves, inserted in an appropriate vessel of edible bread, soaking afloat atop a calm sea. Then an involuntary impulse to illuminate a path towards understanding ignited his mind to fire some flares.

Within his brain, Bastard was able to pursue an internal investigation, interrogate his memories, and search for answers – even as he flirted with a commitment to sleep.

He liked how the bedsheet had chosen its casual coverage of his body. Bastard's eyes were closed, while his open mind made pictures that he couldn't not see: a train; The slobbering sloth; a different city; another typical, unfamiliar hotel. The Abbott, the invisible apartment in the castle. The beating, the pain, the darkness. Charlie sends his best. Just checking in. He had only one stomach. Bastard knew this because he entered into it because the subway entrances had ceased to be and the only way out of town was through Charlie's tummy.

Great darkness. Four stomachs now. The ultimate string quartet. The Abbott did protect him, as he and M.E. had promised.

Dry water. A boat on a river beneath the land. It had been a very long and tiring journey. Why does the river flow East? He couldn't figure it out. Nothing made sense. He was too tired to care. He did care. But he was too tired.

Bastard rubbed a naked leg over Despi's naked legs. The epidermal contact brought him great pleasure.

She was asleep.

Then Bastard was asleep.

PRE-CENTERDAY
(EIGHT)

35

WHAT'S GOING ON.

The next morning, after the second sun had risen, and after a physically attractive intercourse, Bastard went out for the news and returned to bed.

According to supposition, more than 800,00-9 beings in Metropolisse were already on the White Dove. Bastard said nothing because he was reading.

"Yes," Despi confirmed. "It's getting big. Already, the Organization has moved over forty-four thousand cubed kilos of the White Dove. This number will only increase, because that's the kind of number it is. From each addict's VoiceBank...," she trailed off as she tried to do math in her head before remembering, "in total, the Organization is currently bringing in about thirty-three bazillion balls a day. It's a complete success. You should be proud of yourself, and M.E.. You done did good."

Des was talking a lot. Bastard wasn't sure why. He hadn't asked any questions. Even though he was still groggy, he knew that the best way to play this was to just lay there in bed. So he listened, and she went on.

"Our only concern at the moment is keeping up with demand. After all, there is a limited supply of this stuff. Yusef Yusef projects that we will deplete the planet's supply of our pretty little plant within nine lunar cycles – and that's including each moon. Granted, we may be dead by then – but maybe not, seeing as I could be immortal, and you can't stay dead. Anyway, we have to think of the Children..."

Bastard was fully formed when he invested in the best mattress balls available. It was a nice fucking bed. But the more she talked, the more uncomfortable he became.

"M.E. hopes that Diemande will come up with a synthetic substitute...otherwise, we – and everyone who is on the White Dove – will be in a world of shit."

"Interesting..." Bastard farted softly, barely audibly. The air quietly passed through his anus, past both of his butt cheeks, and dissipated beneath the covers of the bed on which they both lay, post-lay. He pinched the bed sheet near where his still enlarged but no longer fully erect penis bulged, lifting the tobacco-silk material up a few inches and bringing it down, repeating this motion a few times until he was satisfied that he had sufficiently dispersed any lingering odor.

She began to snore a bit, but had yet to fall fully asleep. Still slightly a-tremble from their last session, her voice quavered, "What are you thinking, baby?"

Bastard was thinking many things. For example, he didn't understand their relationship, because it made no sense. Why were they seeing each other? What was Des' interest in him? And what was his interest in her? Nah, he understood that. But there were other things... Miguel Evangelista had returned to Metropolisse to testify in court. M.E. contacted and connected with Bastard. M.E.'s got a master plan – to use Free-

Enterprise 999's neo-neuro-chemical radiowave transmission center to push the Organization's new drug, the White Dove. So Bastard made a phone call to F-E 999. Almost immediately after, he met Despi'kha Belle. And then Lance Newcomb, head of F-E 999, hired Bastard as a private detective(!) to follow his wife...who happens to be Bastard's girl from the place. So, not only is Des married to Bastard's arch-enemy, Lance Newcomb, but she's also at least four hundred years old.

Who's actively engaged in battle, here?

"Hmuh? Oh...yeh...sorry." He shifted onto his left side to face her, and looked her in the eyes. She ran her fingers along his back; he flinched ungracefully whenever she touched one of his seven scars, where slightly raised tissue had formed and healed over the seven places he'd been stabbed. Not because the scars were still sensitive, but because the memory of his murder made him shudder...

Bastard leaned in the few inches required for their lips to touch and he kissed her, kindly. He caressed her face with the outside tips of the fingers on his right hand, tracing her cheeks down to her jaw, her neck, her shoulder – all the while keeping his eyes locked on hers. He turned his hand over to touch the soft skin of her upper arm with the printed side of his fingers, and he played a little ditty down her body before holding on her right breast.

"You're beautiful, ..." He led his hand down her torso to her hips, felt her perfect ass in his hand, and moved down to pet the soft bristles of her pubic hair. He pressed his middle finger ever-so-gently into her. "You're still wet," he reported.

"Yes..." she confirmed, and they made love again, for the ninth time that morning.

36

THE FORM-FITTERS EXCEL AT THEIR TASK.

When he reawoke later that afternoon, Des had already left.

After performing his daily rituals, he set out for the Orange Vulture Inc. Manufacturing and Distribution Center to check out and up on the Organization's operation.

The several blocks' walk from his place to the factory was a strange and edifying experience. Bastard felt that he was amongst the walking dead. It was obvious who was on the White Dove and who wasn't, and it seemed to Bastard that nearly everyone was. People moved about aimlessly, sluggishly, happily, ignorantly, obliviously, without sense of purpose or reason or apparent destination. He witnessed four near-deaths of pedestrians who crossed the street with no regard for moving vehicles, barely avoiding mauling. The drivers seemed accustomed to this hazard, actively attending to avoiding them.

He arrived at the plant safely. The store front claimed

a dry cleaning business persisted within. This was false. Bastard walked behind the counter, passed through the Employees Only door, and disappeared into a secret room.

All the manufacturing and distribution of the White Dove happened in the enormous back, which must have taken up half of the block. A Circle there with Dr. Diemande and Yusef Yusef Croniamantal convinced Bastard that everything was proceeding smoothly. He needed confirmation of Despi's report, and he trusted these two, absolutely. They were old confederates; the three of them had worked together on many jobs.

It occurred to Bastard to ask, "So yo – how often has Des been by, since M.E. was taken into 'protective custody.' How has she been doing?"

Both beings answered, "Not once – why?"

"For real? No reason...ai. Thank you, guys. Please keep up the good work."

Bastard left through the front of the front, stepping back out into the outside world.

Lost in his thoughts, he stumbled off the sidewalk, into the street, and almost got hit by a car. He heard four tires screeching and looked up to see a patrol car braking abruptly. It reached a full stop as the bumper brushed up against Bastard's pants.

"Oh, shit," he muttered, "this is fucking perfect..."

Officers Ottoman and Rosalito got out of the car, laughing to each other in their characteristic insidious stupidity.

"Well, well, well – look what we have here!"

"Fucking hell, you can't say one thing that isn't a total fucking cliché," Bastard fumed. "The fuck do you want now? I just got back in town, and I haven't been around long enough to allegedly commit any alleged fucking crimes."

"Well," Rosalito turned to Ottoman and grinned, "You appear to be intoxicated, sir. We saw you stumble out onto the street. You're lucky we didn't run you over. I think it'd be best if we took you in – until you sober up. It's for your own safety, right, yeh. What do you think, partner?"

"Oh yes, of course – for his own safety."

"Because we *care* about your safety, Bastard; we *really* do..."

"You guys make me sick. *You really do*. Have you nothing better to do today than spread your nausea?"

"Not at the moment, no. In fact, we were just on our way to see you. Not only have you saved us the trip, but you've given us a reason to book you. So this really is the best thing we could be doing right now."

Bastard climbed into the back of the cruiser before they had a chance to forcibly and violently inject him therein.

The ride proceeded quietly. It was strange. After a few blocks, they pulled up in front of Apartment Complex 372C – Bastard's place.

"What the f – "

And then it clicked. All three of them burst into uproarious laughter.

"You forgot already, huh *boy*?" she slapped between spasms of ha-ha-has.

"Yes, actually, I did forget. Damn." Bastard sighed. It was a better ending to this episode than he had expected. "So which one of you is who?"

"What, you can't tell?" they giggled together.

"How the fuck could I? – no! You look exactly like Officers Ottoman and Rosalito, and nothing like my friends Sasia Stasia and NNannette Nonet. It's uncanny, for real for real. Let me get a good look at you two."

The two form-fitters turned around in their seats and

offered their fat swollen man mugs for Bastard's inspection.

"Amazing. You two are really talented..."

"Just doing our job, baby – all in a day's work."

"Please, you needn't continue to speak that way – although great work, truly. You really got their mannerisms, and their terribly banal and uninspired cop-talk, down pat. What's going on, though? But wait – first: which one of you is – "

"I'm Sasia..." said Officer Rosalito.

"And I'm still NNannette," said Officer Ottoman.

"Sometimes we switch though; it really doesn't make a difference. None of the boys downtown have noticed anything. And we get to pretend to grill M.E. every day, too, which is -"

"Oh word? How is M.E.?"

"Yup," Rosalito/Stasia confirmed. "You got it. Pretty smart, as always, M.E. is... And he's fine in there, he's good. We can protect him, keep him safe, and keep him informed of everything that's happening on the streets – about the White Dove, about what the Officials are saying and thinking. M.E.'s all right – for now, at least; as long as he stays in our PC."

"Is he really in trouble? With whom?"

"What do you mean? You don't know?"

"How the fuck – what should I – ?"

"Shit. Thought you knew. Evidently, M.E. and Lance Newcomb have done business together in the past. Anyway, Newcomb somehow discovered everything about your plan – he knows what we're doing, he knows about the White Dove. And he's fucking pissed at your boy. So now, Newcomb is not only after you – he's also after M.E.."

"Well, this is great... What the fuck, though? I just saw Des last night, and I asked her -"

"What, on the pier?" Sasia asked. "Dude. We didn't even know you'd be there. So how the fuck did she know? Starting to wonder? Only –"

"Only the Abbott knew, and anyone he or I told. Fuc – "

"K right. I think that when The sloth reported back to Newcomb that you'd disappeared, it was only logical that you were gonna return via the Underground Waterroad. I don't know, brother – but I gotta say, something ain't right with your girl."

"Agreed," NNannette agreed. "We didn't know about that underground river passageway thing between Point West and the City until today. The only people that know about that shit are the Highest Grand Vampires. And honestly fam, none of us have seen Despi since you went West. She has work to do, too, and..."

"Ah, shit. This can't be..."

"What? Why not? Has she mentioned that she's married to Lance Newcomb yet? Has she?"

"No, no – I was waiting to bring it up."

"Well – "

"Ha! What?"

"Seriously, Bastard. Doesn't look good. We seem to have a major problem within the Organization. And it's on you."

"Really doesn't look good, Bastard. Not good."

He sat there in the back seat of the now unmoving car. Looking out and up, he located the window of his office. Something showed motion.

"Fuck me," he whined. "Somebody's up there. Up there in my room."

At that moment, a mediated voice came from a box on the dashboard of the automobile: "All officers in the vicinity of Square 3 and Triangle 9.1: report immediately to Complex 4217D – we have an 88.2-Y2 in progress. All available officers report immediately…"

"That's us – sorry, baby. Duty calls!" smiled Ottoman/ NNannette.

"Think you'll be all right on your own up there?" Rosalito/Stasia asked, nodding to indicate whatever situation awaited Bastard upstairs.

"Ha, yeh, sure, I'll be fine, thank you! Do what you gotta do." Bastard sighed, opened the door, and stepped onto the sidewalk. "And seriously – this is very impressive," he said, making a circle in the air with the tip of his index finger to clarify that he was referring to them and their get-up. He chuckled, "Fucking crazy. Keep up the good work. I'll need to see you two again soon, because I have no idea what's going on. Thanks for the ride, officers." He made a genuine but tired smile before closing the door.

As his friends drove away, Bastard noticed that clouds had re-entered the sky (from the right) and were readying to release the heavy water that inflamed their dark and puffy bodies. Bastard knew that when the sun bleeds, the sun will bleed; and when it weeps, it will weep. There is no denying nature, no matter how hard we try. [1]

1. When the original Weather Conditioners were installed, the People celebrated that civilization had conquered nature. But there were two major flaws in this thinking. First, the reason for the creation and implementation of Weather Conditioners was the death of weather. Civilization hadn't conquered nature - it had killed it. Man-made mechanisms had to be designed to recreate the suddenly extinct phenomena of weather. And although People control these machines, we became no freer, for we continue to be ruled by its established irrational nonconscious forces. By destroying the weather, civilization further enslaved itself to it - because now it had to be managed, cared and worked for. It's like stealing a car that you have to drive all the Time. If you turn off the car, you lose it forever, and you die without a car. Maybe that's not a good analogy. Second, the planet's three suns and two moons became more ferociously independent and

And yet, we continue to try to deny.

Ignoring the torrential downpour, he proceeded to the corner store and picked up some beer. The half-block return walk to his building was enough time for the rain to completely soak through his coat and pants.

A nice night to stay in, he thought to himself, his clothes dripping all over the complex floor. A perfect night for some bourbon, some beer, some...

He took the escalator wing shaft up to his floor, took out his eyeball as he approached his door, and held it in front of the brand new, freshly installed retina scanner that unlocked the door to his apartment.

He entered cautiously, remembering some movement. He felt the curtains breathing, the light changing, the shape of a shadow.

But no one was in his place, and there was nothing out of place. I must be trippin', Bastard said inside his head.

He settled into his desk chair and opened a beer. Taking enormous gulps from the bottle, he finished it within one tenth of a circle and opened another. He spent the next four beers sitting in his chair. He stared out the window and watched the deluge, listening to the shards of silt and the slits of sheer shiny water pummeling the glass panes, wet and gray and obscuring, compromising everything that existed, hiding it and making it somehow no more, as if nothing was more important, because nothing existed. And he thought that he liked this, because he didn't want anything to exist, he wanted nothing to be, he wished everything to be black and empty and dead. It would

overbearing in a deliberate act of defiance in honor of their fallen brothers. So it's a lose-wash scenario.

make everything much simpler. He remembered the darkness of death, and he longed for real peace.

Then he began feeling soothed by the rain, and as he grew calmer, he realized that it was absolutely beautiful. And for the first time in daze, Bastard felt good. He felt all right. He felt as if everything was good, finally. Everything – at least for now – everything was good. Except for the bounty on his and Miguel Evangelista's heads, and except for Despi'kha's dishonesty and potentially malicious intentions, and except for a whole lot of other shit.

But for the moment, for a very brief moment, Bastard felt safe, and good.

37

1. BUT, OF COURSE, NOTHING LASTS FOREVER. MAYBE SOMETHING DOES, BUT I DON'T KNOW ANYTHING ABOUT THAT. 2. BASTARD KILLS THE SLOTH AND BECOMES AN ESCALATOR.

It was on this beautiful, dreadful, and unnecessarily wet evening that The sloth abrupted Bastard and his apartment, breaking down the only doors he'd ever possessed.

When the bangings first sounded, Bastard was still taking a shit. This Time of shit was irregular for him – although it did happen occasionally. Regularly, Bastard shat in the mornings.

So when the knocking first started, Bastard had to finish wiping his ass, which is one chore that he absolutely refuses to rush. He hates ever being rushed in the bathroom; he hates being rushed ever, this is also true. But the increasingly impatient rapping on his front door upset his ability to complete this task with the desired Zen-like calm. He tried his best to relax, and did what needed to be done.

Then he walked over to his desk and back down at his chair sat, trying to think of how to handle this beast best. The pounding on the front door grew more and more forceful and demanding.

Sometimes it's better to postpone the inevitable, especially if you can be using your Time more wisely -- and if not more wisely, less painfully. Plus, Bastard hoped to tire him out a bit before they faced-off.

He cooked up some White Dove and injected it into his butt cheek. Then he prepared an exceedingly healthy amount of dilaudid, which he drew up into the syringe. Fully loaded, he set the needle down upon his desk, and set about looking for some rope.

He thought he had a really good plan.

Instead of rope, Bastard found fishing line, which he had no idea why he had, since he did not fish. He tied it to the desk in the waiting room, first around one leg, then another, then around its body, then around the other legs and then all around again. He pushed the desk closer to the door that led to his office, leaving enough space for that certain special someone to access the door without difficulty.

Then he led the line across the floor, into his office, and closed the door. As tautly as possible, he proceeded to tie it around the doorknob a few hundred times. Then he traced the frame of the door with it, tightly securing the line in place with various glues and adhesives, tape and staples, several times.

Using the scratch tape[1] that he'd found next to the fishing line, which he similarly had no idea (why) he had, Bastard outlined the frame again, sealing the edges

1. I don't think this stuff exists yet - it's tape that ignites when ripped.

of the door to the surrounding frame. Every few fingers, carefully and measuredly, he deposited half a bullet's worth of gunpowder onto the scratch tape before he pressed it down. Next, he removed the hinges that held the door in place.

If The sloth was going to break down the first door, he would probably immediately break down the second one. And this could be a lot of fun to watch.

He picked up the syringe and taped it in the palm of his left hand in such a way that the needle stuck out between his middle and ring fingers.

Then he down back behind his desk sat.

Bastard didn't have to wait long before the behemoth succeeded in breaking through the first door and into the waiting room adjacent, slurping and slurring and splurging and sputtering whilst serving a slew of profanities.

Moments later, The sloth was at the second door, the one to Bastard's office. He held his breath in anticipation. Somewhat surprisingly, but not that interestingly, the filthy giant primate tried the handle.

After all that shit, Bastard had forgotten to lock the door.

He watched as an invisible hand of pudgy turds turned the doorknob from the other side.

But The sloth didn't convince the door to open; the tape was holding it in place. Instead of merely applying greater force (pushing a little harder – scratch tape isn't that strong), The sloth sounded retreating, grumbling and gurgling, before charging the door with his mass.

What ensued was truly comical, though Bastard didn't have enough room to laugh.

The sloth broke down the door with relative ease. The tearing of the scratch tape ignited the gunpowder deposits. As the big sweaty ape crashed through the door, the serial barrage of gun claps sent the monster reeling, blindly taking cover from what he must have assumed were bullets directed at him.

The waiting–room–desk–tethered–to–office–door booby trap failed – but only because it was a terrible idea and made no physical sense. (The string broke and the desk stayed in place.) Fortunately, however, somehow the fishing line tripped up the gargantuan, sending him to the floor atop the door that splintered beneath his incredible weight.

The sloth groaned gloriously and farted fluently. Bastard quickly stepped to him and repeatedly kicked his face with a steel-toed blue velvet Vaseline boot that he found on his right foot. He stopped after six or nine punts.

Then he ripped off the tape around the syringe in his palm. He had planned to plant his first punch with a carefully timed tightening of the fist, so that the base of his palm would push the plunger down and shoot the dope into his attacker upon contact.

Instead, Bastard simply bent down and injected The sloth good and well full. The whale of lard passed a moan through its blowhole and presently went limp.

Bastard returned to his desk and sighed as he sat down again. He poured himself a big glass of grain and started working on it. He needed to collect his thoughts and make sure he was all present and accounted for.

His brain-fingers flipped through his mind's files on the Organization's Friends and Family as he considered who could best help him in this specific situation. Naturally, he wanted the Cleaner and the Interior Decorator. In terms of getting rid of corpses and all other criminal incriminates, these two made the best team. Unfortunately, they were presently unavailable, having gone on vacation after falling in love with each other on their last job.

There were others who could help, but Bastard's ruminations began to diffuse. Miguel Evangelista wasn't around, and he felt a sudden need to talk to M.E.. They hadn't communicated since Moonday, when he left for Point West. A lot of shit had gone down since then. He needed to see his boy.

His thoughts continued to spread out amongst his peoples. As soon as the name Despi'kha occurred within, his attention coalesced on her. But further mental pursuit was interrupted by the telephone, which once again began to make that noise. He thought about answering it; then he did.

He picked up the ear piece, and before he could say anything, a voice sounded in his ear and demanded, "What's happening, why haven't you reported yet? What's going on up there? Just tie him up and bring the motherfucker down to the car already – unless you've killed him, in which case – "

Bastard looked out the window and down at the street. There was a black van parked in front of the building. He coughed into the phone, grunted and grumbled in the gruffest growl he could gather, "I'll grow right down."

He hung up the phone and thought. He couldn't be sure that his impersonation of The sloth was convincing, and he questioned his own word choice. He had to move fast. Well, maybe not too fast, because they were waiting on The sloth. Bastard figured this graced him with some small circles of space before they'd send reinforcements.

There was no way for Bastard to physically impersonate the blubbering blob. And there was no way he could carry that overweight walrus down to the street on his own – nor could he see any reason to. He looked down at the steaming pile of human-ish shit splayed on his floor, then he looked out the window again. Two heavily dressed people emerged from the van and walked to the entrance of his building.

Okay, he thought. *Time to go.*

Bastard grabbed his balls and gathered other immediate necessities in a sack: blade, tobacco, White Dove, business cards, Glock 21, lighter, dynamite, pipe, ass wipes, two pocket grenades, socks, a nice bottle of wine in case he had to stay at a friend's place, antihistamines and methamphetamines. Some of the latter he crushed up and blasted. He knew he would have to move and think quickly, and he actually believed this would help.

He didn't want to leave The sloth spread dead in his office, but he didn't have Time to hide the body, set it on fire, or ritually disembowel and/or decapitate him. His main concern was returning to the smell of the rotting cadaver, but considering how foully the fucker's fumes filled the air when he was alive, Bastard concluded that it couldn't possibly get worse.

He walked on the doors, through the open door frames, into the hallway.

Down the hall, he saw the numbers above the escalator wing shaft tick up as his enemies approached the 33rd. Bastard hurried in the other direction. He made it around the corner and out of sight just as the audible *ding* signified a stop.

"Let's go," said a voice he couldn't recognize. Then he sensed a silent acknowledgment that he thought felt familiar. Bastard wanted to peek around the corner to see who it was, but decided not to risk it.

"Wait here for a sec, I'm,a check it out first." Then,

STEFAN O. RAK

a few moments later, "Holy fuckshit! The sloth is dead.
Bastard ain't here. You can come in."

He listened as the second person dialed some
numbers on a personal cellephonic device while
entering Bastard's apartment, stepping on broken
pieces of door and kicking away debris.

"Hey babe, we got a situation here." It was Lance
fucking Newcomb talking – probably to Despi'kha
fucking Belle? "Keep an eye on the exits down there.
The sloth is dead, and Bastard isn't here. He's probably
still in the building, on his way out. We gotta find him."

Bastard had to get to the basement; from there, he
could exit via the loading storage furnace garbage area.

As quietly and quickly as he could, he danced down
the corridor to the escalator wing-shaft like the pitter
patter of rain on a windshield, avoiding the wipers that
could knock him down onto the floor. He pressed the
button over-determinedly and the doors opened. Once
inside, he depressed a different round circular piece of
plastic in order to send the moving machine to the
basement. He hit that button a hundred times, it
seemed, before the metal doors finally closed. The
descent took hours. When the lift finally stopped,
Bastard realized he was perspiring. Taking his
handkerchief from his back right pocket, he mopped his
brow and the back of his neck. He neatly refolded it.
The doors had already opened; as he was replacing his
handkerchief, the doors began to close.

He pressed the Door Open button, frantically, again
and again he pressed that Door Open button – to no
effect, for the doors had closed. Then the lift began to
ascend. Nervously, he fingered every button between
the basement and the 33rd – and though these buttons
lit up, the mover denied each request. Bastard needed to
get off this certain death trap. He knew that Newcomb

and his partner were controlling the lift, summoning it back to them. This could be the end of him, he knew, he thought, and thinking about this made him sweat even more...

Bastard cursed himself for not taking Despi's dishonesty more seriously; he'd been away for two days – and upon his return, she's lying to him about nearly everything. Sasia Stasia and NNannette Nonet confirmed that M.E. was locked up somewhere. But why did Des tell him that she'd been to the warehouse, that everything was proceeding smoothly and according to plan, when she hadn't been in touch with anyone. It seemed like a stupid and unnecessary lie. He should have recognized that something was amiss, that she had betrayed him, or just straight fucked him.

Had she planned to fuck him over from the start?

At the moment, it didn't really matter...and yet it did matter. He loved her, evidently – and it took this betrayal to make him realize the depth and the power of what that truly meant. Would it have played out differently had he professed his love for her to her? Could he have kept her on, or converted her to, his side? Maybe she had no choice, and Newcomb was forcing her under threat. But he couldn't accept that. We all make our own choices. If she loved him as much as he loved her, she wouldn't set him up like this... And she – she was his enemy, then, too. Bastard cringed at the thought.

Curiously, he wasn't disappointed with himself for falling for her; she was too beautiful, too perfect, to be to blame. To not have fallen into her trap would have been a slight against humankind; no, he couldn't blame himself, and he couldn't blame her.

More than any other identifiable emotion, Bastard felt a depressive, overpowering disappointment oppressively weighing upon him like a thick cloak of iron, pushing him down to the ground, too heavy to stand up against. He was losing the ability to stand up straight...his body, empty of all that made man human, could no longer hold his flesh and bones in place...and he began to fold in upon himself, his body buckling beneath him, crumpling up into a ball, just as one scrunches up a thin piece of paper before tossing it in the trash.

Bastard's heart was beating too fast. His chest was a constricting leaden vise; he clutched his breast and pressed upon it, the physical pressure temporarily alleviating the negative side effects of love and meth. With great effort, he pushed himself up off the floor of the escalator – which, he just realized, had come to a stop.

The doors opened, and he was no longer on the escalator. He was an escalator.

CENTERDAY (NINE)

38

NO BROWN GOO FOR BREAKFAST FOR BASTARD, THANK YOU!

When Bastard awoke, he felt alone. He knew his body would be heavy if he tried to move it. He ached stiff and crusty, which made him think of a dirty rag that had dried over a clothesline in the cold.

He didn't have to open his eyes to know that he was in an unfamiliar place...he tried opening them...it was eleven forty thirteen...he didn't recognize anything between his sagging leaden eyelids...but he did not feel threatened, he wasn't scared...he looked at the Circlekeeper again...it was twelve sixty nine...another twenty little circles and I'll get up, he thought to himself...another twenty, thirty, and I'll get up...

And he slept some more.

He dreamed about *a place, a vast green grassen land, and there were structures there, big structures, large buildments of steel and iron and metal soft metal fabrics that lay upon the land but were soft to the touch like lamb's steel wool...and he tossed and he turned as he dreamt of a jungle, he was taking a shower even though he was clean, and there was a serpent there that graced the ceiling and could extend the length of many yards, apparently hovering in space, and he knew he had to kill somebody, he didn't mind having to kill somebody but he didn't know why it had to be done, and anyway he thought the guy was all right; but he knew that he had to do what he had to do. There was a pool there, and the snake might be in it. The boat was about to leave, and if he didn't catch it, he knew he would be stuck there forever. The boat became a barge, and he was on it, and the barge began its descent down the river. He observed a great and beautiful black bird soaring, except he didn't even see it flying, he only saw it falling helplessly from the sky as if its wings no longer worked, no longer served their purpose, no longer serviced the bird in enabling aviation...the bird was losing its beauty as it fell towards the earth...when it left the sky, it hit the river and entered the water. Piranhas swarmed its body, ripping its flesh apart. In less than a blind blink, there was no more bird. Feathers floated down the river, first in bloody bunches, then drifting apart, carried away by the various currents...warm blood flowed from the black bird's wounds, forming a pool of dark red within the river, which then became distinct streams within the stream. The blood that flowed into the river almost surpassed the size of the bird itself in volume – but then as the sanguine veins continued to extend and expand, the dead bird started to grow. And as it grew and grew, the blood came more and more quickly, its output increasing with each beat of Bastard's trembling heart. For the river was now completely red, and the body of the bird now stretched across the entire river, from one bank to the other, a limp carcass bridge. Bastard watched as some drifting branches and leaves reached the gigantic avian corpse and lodged against its flank, pushing against it, held in place by the insistent determination of the water's course. Above, the river held clean and clear, cool, fresh water; below: a steaming, thick, hot and red muddy bloody ooze.*

When he woke up this Time, he realized that he was covered in blood. He sat up with a start, aghast, and nervously began feeling his body for wounds, trying to locate the source of the blood. But apart from various painful bruises and other injuries he'd survived over the previous circles, he found no new injuries.

The sheets were wet, so he threw them off his body. He stood up and ventured into the bathroom adjacent to this bedroom. He didn't recognize this place at all, and had no recollection of getting there. But for some reason, he did not feel threatened; he felt comfortable, and safer than he had for quite some Time. He took a leisurely, lengthy, lukewarm shower, which combined the benefits of a searingly hot shower and a scathingly cold shower and resulted in a sense of both relaxation and reinvigoration alongside cleanliness of both mind and body.

After scrubbing himself thoroughly with the cactus loofah and soaping himself through with a new bar of tech wax, he turned off the water, doused himself in absinthe, then stepped out of the basin and dried himself off with some aromatic bitters he found on the rack.

He found a set of clothes in the toilet bowl, which fit him perfectly, though they weren't his size – in fact, they were much too small. But he felt good. He shaved with some curdled butter and a toothpick, and sprayed deodorant on his face. For the first time in years, he felt hungry.

A pleasing aroma came to his nostril hairs, the scent traveling from somewhere in this foreign apartment or house or whatever he was in to the bedroom bathroom. When he was all dressed and ready, he set off to find the source of the smells.

The apartment was small, with only two rooms, but the hallway that connected the bedroom to the open kitchen/living room was the length of a dough-ball field – five thousand neckties. The smell of cooking, the sounds of steaming and frying, teased his already asking stomach.

Entering the kitchen, which shared the same blue-orange Venus fly trap motif as the bedroom and the interminable hallway, he found some pots and pans on the stove: scrambled young roe with carrot ginger cuticles sizzling in first cold pressed extra anal virgin scrapple gas in one; another with fried armadillo bacon, perfectly crispy; and in the next, something brown that he didn't recognize, which did not smell appetizing at all. He took a couple of pieces of carpet from the toaster, still hot to the touch, and utilized them to devour the contents of two of the pans, leaving the last one, the unappetizing brown goo, untouched. Having had his fill, he went to the living room and sat down on the only couch, a mustard yellow loveseat, and waited for something to happen.

After some Time passed, and nothing happened, he decided that it must be about then to move on. Re-generated, re-fueled, re-started, he grabbed a coat that hung on a hook by the front door and exited the apartment.

Upon closing the door behind him, he realized exactly where he was – he was on Addition Street, only a few blocks away from his own place...but what kind of apartment like that just leads out onto the street? And who the fuck lives there – whose place was it?

He turned and looked back at the front door, which

did not appear as it did moments ago when he'd exited through it. No, decidedly not: it was very different. He found himself standing in front of an enormous 38-story luxury condominium of blue glass and jade marble; a doorman asked him if he deserved a taxi?

"Where the fuck did you come from?" Bastard demanded.

The man disappeared.

Perplexed, Bastard decided to take the Air Train home, which would take much longer than if he walked, to try and collect his thoughts...piece together the events of the previous night(s). He had no idea how long he had been unconscious or asleep – it could have been days.

39

BASTARD INVITES HIMSELF TO A PARTY.

When the Air Train pulled into the station, an image of elevator doors closing flashed behind him round. He jumped aboard, found some space, and held onto the ceiling handrail.

"There are a hundred serial killers running loose in this great city, and you don't know who anyone is – it could be anyone – I mean, anyone could be – look around, man! No one pays any attention to anything at all anymore – all on their message machines, constantly, chips in their heads, busy communicating with other non-present automatons, blindly bumbling down the blocks, in one borough but communicating to another in some other hood – not even looking up when they cross the street – and these, these serial killers – they're on the loose – it's in the fucking *news* –, taking one life each a day – and you-you do nothing?"

Two youngish – but not young enough – hipsters carelessly shared their conversation.

"What do you suggest? Huh? I continue living my –"

" – careful there, you don't have a – "

"But what the fuck? We none of us has any idea when or how we're going to die – at least – but I can always do the only thing I can do, until I no longer can't. Who gives a shit – I don't mean that, quite – but ultimately, finally, what's the difference if it's a serial killer or a car or a heart attack or a cancer seizure or overdosing on the White Dove?"

"They say you can't overdose on the White Dove..."

"Yeh, I've heard that. I hope it's true. But who knows. It hasn't been around long enough for anyone to really know... I mean, come on...where did this shit come from? Both the Kingdom's Official Department on Drugs and the IDC have nothing – there's no literature. Nothing! It's pretty crazy, if – "

"Have you tried it? The White Dove?"

"What do you – I mean, I thought everyone has; – why, haven't you?"

"Well...no, not yet...no."

"Really?"

"Yeh...really..."

"Neither have I, actually."

"Really?" Pause. He looked around the cabin of the car; Bastard feigned disinterest. "Well... Hey listen: I hear there's a party tomorrow night – my buddy was talking about it, saying it should be a dope fucking party, no pun intended, hahahahahaha. Tomorrow night at eleven o'clit, at the old Green Warehouse on Third and E. You ever been there? I hear they have wild fucking parties over – "

"Wait a second – yeh, tomorrow night, right? I think I did hear something about this, for real–"

"For real?"

"Yeh man – for real, yeh. Axis was talking about this crazy fucking party – tomorrow night – but over on

Avenue F, he was saying – and yeh so, you wanna go? Should we go? I'm down, if you – "

Bastard was cringing in pain from their voices, their names, their conversation. He was growing increasingly distressed, but he wanted to find out how much these idiots knew about the White Dove. And, of course, he wanted to know where the party was. Was it on E or F?

"I'm down, let's fucking go!"

"All right man, should be fun!"

"You have my identity code sequence, right? Mental me the address now so I have it, okay – before you forget...and before I forget – so I don't have to remind you...to remind me, okay?"

"I just did it. You get it?"

Bastard watched as the other young man pulled a small DigiB Sheet out of his right front pocket and held it up, near eye level, so that it could read the address that he'd just received. "Yeh I got it, it's right here man, thanks." Bastard was at just the right angle to peer over the triangular body of the kid and read the address off the screen. It seemed as though the other dude noticed Bastard's curious peeping – he did have to stand a bit on his toes in order to get a full view of the screen – but I couldn't be certain. In any case, the young men had reached their destination and disembarked the Air Train.

Bastard sat down, quietly incognito in his beaded aquamarine beard and ostrich-beige ostrich sunglasses, and attempted to process the dialogue he had just overheard. Many thoughts bugled and bungled about his bastardly mind. Almost all of them dissipated into the thinnest of air and died alone forgotten thoughts, forever irretrievable and inadmissible in court.

Then, for no reason, Bastard said out loud, "I'm gonna go to that party."

40

BASTARD GOES TO JAIL.

There were many things that Bastard did not like about incarceration; although not on the top of this list, visiting loved ones in jail was close.

Sasia Stasia as Officer Rosalito and NNannette Nonet as Officer Ottoman met Bastard at the precinct. Their guidance and company would ease the unpleasantness of the security process. They led Bastard through a series of metal-, steel-, glass-, iron-, flaxion-, bagelnisse-, and vitriglu-detectors; past the security dogs; past the drug-sniffing police officers (No Petting, No Sudden Movements); and finally the strip-and-swim.

"Thank you, my loves," Bastard sneezed as Stasia/Rosalito handed him two towels to dry off. "Your presence alone makes this so much more bearable than it would otherwise be." He wrapped a towel around his waist and tossed the other one over his shoulders, where it fell partly resting atop his crown.

Sasia and NNannette laughed. "Think nothing of it, Bastard – "

" – if not less," they all chimed in together, and laughed again.

But the laughter fell hard upon the concrete, cold and solid and gray. Even considering the relative comfort of the security screening process, the fact remained that Bastard was still visiting his beloved homie in jail.

"But it's not really jail, Bastard – you must remember that. He's simply being held here for his own protection."

"True. True." The three continued walking down a long, narrow corridor, passing countless office doors and countable uniform-clad automatons (Bastard counted seven thus far). "I'm sorry, but fuck that. It's still Grand Central Station Holding."

"I know, but trust us. M.E.'s not in population – hasn't even been charged with anything. The man is simply too important for this case; and it's too important to the Nation – and to their lawyers – to risk having Miguel on the outside."

"Whatever it means, that's what they are saying. He's earned a lot of enemies over this."

"Yeah, you mean by ratting on Newt Humbert? He's gained a bunch of new enemies??? Narcing on a dude who doesn't exist? What friends can Newt Humbert have? This is bullshit."

"You'd be surprised," Stasia/Rosalito answered. "I certainly was. Fucking assholes go crazy over a cause. And motherfuckers take sides. More importantly, it's not the friends of N.H., but the enemies of M.E.. And let's face it: nobody likes a rat. Even if nobody knows who the rattee is (or whether or not he even exists). And"

"But more than anything, B, it's Lance Newcomb. He's

behind all of the threats, as far as we can tell – at least all of the serious threats. The less-serious threats can be pretty hilarious, actually; I heard – "

Seeing that Bastard was not going to be easily amused, Nonet/Ottoman let her/his voice trail off. Bastard grumbled something unintelligible that everyone understood.

When they finally reached the door to M.E.'s room, Bastard tried to release some tension: "Well, that was by far the most pleasant journey I've ever had passing through prison security to visit a friend on the inside. Now, if you don't mind, I would like my clothes back. I'm all dry," he concluded, taking off the towels and handing them to Stasia/Rosalito, who pressed them against the fabric of the uniform upon her stomach with crossed forearms. Nonet/Ottoman handed Bastard his clothes. While he re-dressed, she knocked on the door three times and coughed nine times. Between the third and sixth expectorations, Stasia/Rosalito jingled some keys out of her pocket and entered a code that opened the door to Miguel Evangelista's cell.

"We can't wait outside for you, baby – official business, ha, for real. But we'll come back as soon as we can, aight?" Bastard wasn't sure if it was aight, so he said nothing.

He squeezed through the open door-hole and entered the small room slowly. Miguel Evangelista turned around in his seat. Bastard heard the door clank shut behind him, and the echoes of his escorts' shoe-steps faded into the past tense.

41

KEEP YOUR EYES ON THE EYEBALLS (IS GOOD ADVICE EVEN IF YOU AREN'T INTO SPORTS).

"Fucking hell man it's good to see you," Bastard splurged.

M.E. rose from his seated position at a desk in the far corner of the room and grinned. "Welcome to my new digs, Bastard. I know it's not much," he said, extending his arms and turning a bit to the right and then to the left, "but it really ain't all that bad. And it's good to see you, too."

Bastard smiled in accordance and approached his old friend with arms outstretched, in preparation for a hug.

"No no no – don't do that, bro. They got cameras in here, they'll think you're giving me something. And honestly, I hope you didn't bring me anything; I have everything I could possibly need already. Unless you brought M.E. something – did you???"

"All right man, sorry about that – and nah, fam. Didn't bring shit. Anyway, I thought this was a cushy spot – the 'No Touching' rule wouldn't apply. Whatever. Not important. Just trying to show a brother some love."

Bastard looked around the room. M.E. had a bed in one corner; a toilet in the other, by the door. Against the back wall to the right was a sizable concrete desk, with a brand-new computer, a desk lamp, paper, pencils, erasers, white out (what for?), scotch tape, stapler, post-it notes, and so on. A program was running on the computer; a rapid series of digits and figures continued to fleet across the screen as Bastard decided upon a place to plant his behind. He settled on the bed, settling his ass on M.E.'s bed.

He both inhaled and exhaled.

"So tell Bastard, M.E.: what the fuck is going on?"

M.E. laughed out loud – louder than intended, judging by his immediate regainsure of composing. Then he began to say words, shakily, as if he had just learned them.

"Oh brother. *What is going on?* What *is* goin' on. What is goin' *on*! What *is going* on? What *is going on!?!* What is goin' on?" Stutter, moment. M.E. appeared confused. Bastard was worried, and then confused as well. M.E. restartled: "You tell me," and tried very hard to look at Bastard, blankly. Bastard had never heard M.E. use that word before... "You tell me, man: tell me what's going on?" And again.

Bastard failed to comprehend. "That's what I'm asking you, man; what is going on? You tell *me*. What's happening with the trial? What's happening with you – I mean, are you all right? For real for real – y'aight?'

Miguel Evangelista's eyes seemed to shift within his face. "Yes."

A heavy dread and panic overcame Bastard as he realized that now both he and M.E. were locked up.

"Tha fuck is up with you? Listen fam, I stopped by

Orange Vulture's warehouse the other day – production and distro and shit is going fine there. White Dove sales are strong and going up. But otherwise – fuck man, crazy shit went down since I last saw you. Fuckers be tryin' to kill your brother every fuckin' day. We gotta talk about...Despi'kha is...aw man, the trip out West – I saw the Abbott...you hear about my escape through the underground river, right? But I can't even explain that, and I can't tell you what happened last night, because even I don't fucking know... Except that I killed The motherfucking sloth! That's right! He dead! But dude, I'm,a be dead, too – and soon. Newcomb keeps upping the bounty on my head. And I never was the best fighter. I didn't mind dying the first Time – but I do enjoy life, because I have wonderful friends."

Nothing.

"Aaaccchhh, will you please talk to a brother, man? What the fuck is going on? And if you can't tell me what's going on, then let Bastard tell M.E. what's been goin' on, so we can try to figure this fucking shit out. Because it's fucked up, man. I need your help. I'm just hoping that everything is cool with you. And on our side. I trust Yusef Yusef Yusef Croniamantal, and Dr. Diemande. I trust our people – they're family. And I can't understand what you're doing here. And Despi's fucking...I mean, shit doesn't make sense. Maybe it does, and I just don't wanna learn." Bastard paused. He thought he might cry a bit, but he didn't. "And what's this I hear about you having worked with Lance Newcomb before? Since when you don't level with your boy, with your partner?? You holdin' out on me, M.E.?"

Bastard remembered that Despi was his source for that information. She had told him that Miguel Evangelista had worked with Lance Newcomb before. All Bastard needed was for his brother to confirm or deny, which M.E. would definitely do, depending on whether it was true or not. M.E. said nothing.

"So – what?" Bastard barked sharply, thrusting his arms out quick and puffing his chest. But as he staccatoed those two words, he had his eyes on M.E..

He hadn't realized it, but he had felt it as soon as he entered the room. He recognized the appearance and the shape of his long-time compatriot, but he didn't feel the warmth that Miguel naturally generated; indeed, M.E. was cold.

Yet strangely enough, Miguel Evangelista's long, black hair glistened with sweat – no; no. His hair wasn't glistening...it appeared to be melting...growing fatter, thicker, longer, then bulbous in certain areas, only to shrink, withdraw, smooth out, like thick globs of sludge sliding up and down, except thin, because I'm describing the man's hair...

And his face tended to sag as he spoke no words...it would elongate and retract... And his eyes grew wide whenever he said anything, as if he was startled by his own speech. But now, the man was silent.

Bastard knew his friend well, and he knew that this appeared to be the body of his brother, Miguel Evangelista. But with every third tick, he felt a twinge of uncertainty that grew into definite conviction. He decided that this was not his friend. But two out of three almost sufficed...if for no other reason than that Bastard *wanted* to believe; he *wanted* this to be M.E., he wanted to be *talking* to M.E., he wanted answers to questions that only M.E. could answer unquestionably.

The machine sputtered. Miguel's eyes starting growing exceedingly large for his face – only to nearly disappear, then reappear again; his nose drifted upward only to reappear in place; his five facial features figuratively flew and re-positioned in disproportionate disparate displacements.

"All right," Bastard drew a deep breath, unsure of where the following line of inquiry would take him, but fairly certain that he wouldn't like it. "What the fuck is going on? Who – or what – are you? Where is Miguel Evangelista? What have you done with him?" Bastard was getting angrier and more impatient by the split-circle. He was now certain that this wasn't the real M.E. – it was either a fake or a robot android impersonation or a virtual recreation or someone else in a Miguel Evangelista costume. Yes, there was something markedly mechanical about this facsimile of a friend...

Bastard's suspicions were justified when a small stream of mechanical steam began to emanate from the thing's rubber ears.

At which point the door to the cell suddenly burst open. Officers Rosalito and Ottoman charged into the room and slugged Bastard on the top of the head with their clubs. Bastard lost consciousness, his limp body collapsing on the cold, gray ground of the cell.

42

WHEN NO ONE IS THERE TO ASK, IF YOU ASK NO ONE, THERE IS ONLY PART OF THE PROBLEM THAT IS THERE.

If a day passes, what has happened? Do we know? I certainly do not.

Bastard wakes up.

His eyes faze, gluey mists a lens glaze; his head hurting a blaze.

He remembers stomach.

He remembers thinking that he was thirsty, and remembers that he was thirsty.

He sinks into the cement.

Clangs come.

Kicks in the stomach.

In the dark he tries to get up; coughing; more kicks and he stays down a.

The   lights   go   out: nd click.........click.........click.........clang.

Clang.

Quiet.
And always the darkness.
And then the light.
And they both hurt.

43

BASTARD'S CELL MATE SPEAKS.

Another kick in the stomach.

"Fuck off," Bastard groaned.

"What gratitude!!! Hmph. What's that old saying – 'No good idea goes without being punished by its own specific level of eternal suffering'?"

"Oh man...seriously? That's ridiculous." He looked up at an old man who was loosely dressed in rags that barely hinted at their original purpose as articles of clothing. The old man shook his head in response to Bastard's head shaking.

"So what's your good idea, then, man?" Bastard's body sore, he lolled back and forth on the floor in order to build up enough momentum to get up. He managed to succeed, got onto his hands and knees, and pushed himself up with great pain and difficulty.

"I was told to wake you and so I did."

"Okay, good idea. Good job, old man." Bastard looked around, groggy at first and then wide awake – "Fuck there's a bed here? How long was I out on that cold hard floor?"

"You're not asking the right questions. This is getting boring. You know I can have any roommate I want!"

"No, I didn't know that – how would I have known that. Shit you are old. How old are you?"

"Older than that."

"Your hair is a suggestion, and your skin looks used. What are you in for? And what the fuck does that mean, I can have any roommate I want? Roommate? How long you been here? The fuck did you do?"

"Doesn't matter what I did. What matters is what you have to do, my son. This is not a real prison. You're in Lance Newcomb's private basement dungeon. I've been here for...for far too long, if not forever. But you – you can leave. And you must leave. Soon."

"You're insane, old man."

"Immaterial. He will come for you. He said that he would come for you. I saw him, and I saw him when he came out of the floor."

"I can't believe I've been sleeping on the concrete when there's an empty fucking bed – there's a bed for me here?!?"

"They are not nice people."

"What the fuck are you talking about?"

A loud metallic bang and the lights went on and lots of voices began shouting eagerly.

"Feed time," the old man hissed. "Don't eat it. Those who do, die faster. Not nicer, either. If you don't accept anything they give you, you may have a chance. If you want to die here, satisfy your hunger. If you want to take Newcomb down, though, you must live a little longer."

Bastard collapsed on the lower bunk. The little old hunchback screamed something about the lower bunk being his bunk and that Bastard's was up top...but he was soon asleep again, and did not dream about the old man's concerns.

"Wake up, wake up. It's time to go."

Bastard moaned. Everything hurt.

Something grabbed his leg and pulled. He fell out of bed onto the floor. He turned his head and made eye contact with two other eyes in a man's face. The man's face was dirty, and he wore a lamp on his forehead, overtop a yellow skullcap. He seemed to have no body. Just a head, coming out of the cell floor.

"Suck on this." The head produced an arm with a hand that held a tube to Bastard's mouth. He inhaled and immediately woke up. "Get the fuck down here, now." Another arm appeared and a man crawled out of the cement. "Now go down into that hole. There's a tunnel that will take you the fuck out of here."

"Can someone tell me what the fuck is going on? I'm a little lost."

"No time, no time!" the old man spat everywhere. "Ungrateful ingrate."

"Listen, man – you better get the fuck down there before I change my mind," said the dude in the yellow skully.

"How does that make sense?"

"It's me or you, man. I'm doing this for the greater good of the Organization. I'm one of your men, Bastard. There are two men in this cell. So there can't be only one – we need another body to take your place. They count bodies here – future corpses, they call 'em. I came here because I agreed to trade places with you. I am staying, because you are going. You have to break into the Newcomb Estate Compound. You have to steal the Refleshing Brick Sphere or some shit like that. So go and do what you gotta go do."

44

I REMEMBER A STORY THAT BASTARD ONCE TOLD ME, ABOUT M.E.. HE TOLD ME NOT TO TELL ANYONE. IT WAS A GOOD STORY, THOUGH.

When the sun shines in certain areas, it is known to not shine in others. Even on a planet with three suns, there are always two places where one sun does not shine.

The first thing that popped into Bastard's mind upon the suggestion of escape was Despi.

He imagined her sharp eyes and soft skin, her face lighting the way as he crawled through the wet, dark tunnel for hours, maybe days.

The other thing to consider is that even with three suns, there are always two places where no sun ever shines.

POST-CENTERDAY
(TEN)

45

'DAY ALWAYS TURNS INTO NIGHT' IS NOT TRUE HERE, BUT NOT BECAUSE THERE ARE THREE SUNS AND TWO MOONS.

The tunnel led him to let him out above ground at the old factory yards by the river, where he and the Mechanic used to meet. The crib wasn't far away. He limped his way home without incident.

Bastard knew that the guards wouldn't notice his absence until the following morning – if then. So he took care to clean himself and his wounds, and dress himself and his wounds.

After he was done with all of that, he sat at his desk. In his chair, where he was most comfortable. Bastard practiced performing a purposeful pose and pondered.

It was the day before the final hearing of the trial of the case of the Kingdom of the Nation vs. Newt Humbert, in which M.E. was the principle witness for the prosecution, and Bastard hadn't seen M.E. since the last time they had met.

That was right before his trip West to meet the

Abbott. He had managed to escape back East through the Underground River, after successfully navigating the string quartet cow stomachs. He had met with a weird robotic like fake Miguel Evangelista, but that doesn't count. Many things had happened. And many things would happen. And these things would make a difference.

Bastard thought about what he should do. He knew something had to be done, and considered many courses of action, formulated many plans and many possible scenarios and many even unimaginable resolutions. He wondered what would be best for the Organization, for the White Dove, for his Crew. He wondered where the fuck was M.E.? Only so much time existed between what was then now and the following day.

Without an audible footstep, the sound of a knock on the door, or even the hint of a draft, Miguel Evangelista opened the door to Bastard's office, entered the room, and closed the door behind him.

"What tha fuck?" Bastard inquired.

M.E. replied by approaching Bastard's desk, setting a brown textile briefcase upon the surface between them, and opening it to pull out a stack of papers.

Without looking at the dossier, Bastard nodded in incomprehension. "What are we talkin' about?"

"Remember we spoke about breaking into Lance Newcomb's compound?" was the first thing M.E. said.

Bastard did not remember this conversation, and said, "No. I don't remember that conversation." He picked up the stack of papers, didn't know why, and replaced it. "But I believe you. In fact, I was just thinking about breaking into Newcomb's place. I just didn't know what to steal."

"Makes sense," Miguel Evangelista accepted. "Listen

very closely, Bastard. Every con knows that this asshole Lance Newcomb possesses a legendary, mythical collection of things. Ancient artifacts, objects, archives, sacred texts, rookie's hearts, shiny rocks, machines from the future. All invaluable, irreplaceable, irreproducible; many inexplicable, indecipherable, inarticulate, even inarticulable. Tokens, totems, treasures, creations, products – all from other worlds, other Times, other realities. He keeps them all on the third floor of his Estate. The whole floor is like an incredible museum – a museum full of things that prove that so many things we think we know are not true at all. It's a total mind-fuck, supposedly, and there are few minds that are capable of surviving the experience of seeing all of this mind-blowing stuff. You, Bastard, may be the first of very few mind potentials who can get in there and get out a..."

"Where the fuck have you been, dude?" Bastard interjected.

M.E. ignored the question. "We all know the legend about the cat who broke into the Lance Newcomb Estate without knowing what to steal..."

"I don't know that story, man," Bastard admitted. Then he thought to ask, "What the fuck is going on?"

M.E. ignored that question, too. "Let M.E. explain the story's relevance. Now, you must take into account that this occurred before Newcomb's agency installed environmental protections around the Estate. You'll learn about these soon.

"Anyway, this cat broke into the mansion and made it to the third floor. His plan was simply to grab what he could and split. But while browsing the exhibition of Newcomb's improbable goods, he was so overwhelmed by the magnitude and grandeur and vastness of the collection that he entered into a trance or something.

Possibly induced by the brilliance of the reflections of the bright lights upon the precious stones and metals that did not exist, or the depth of the meaning of the art that was never made. The impossibility of the objects around him and the inexplicability of their place in his world. Maybe he was gassed. But dude was so mesmerized that he became incapacitated. Mentally. He didn't know what to steal, and he got stuck. Psychologically paralyzed of purpose, he was physically paralyzed. And to this day, you can still see him there: the burglar who tried to steal from Lance Newcomb. For he is still there, frozen in form, on the third floor of the Newcomb Estate, as one of the private museum's acquisitions."

Bastard looked at his friend and replied, "Thank you. Why are you telling me this? Are we just talking about it, or are we talkin' about it?"

M.E. replied, "Well, now we talkin' about it. Because, my brother, now we know what to steal. There is something in Newcomb's possession, that he keeps in his collection. Highly protected and possibly impossible to locate, get to, and remove, this one object is the key to Newcomb's immortality. If you succeed in this mission, you will hold Lance Newcomb's life in your hands, literally. You need to get in there and steal this shit tonight."

At that moment, Sasia Stasia entered the room. She knew Bastard's place well and she came quickly in comfortably.

"Fuck," she succumbed to the wood-cushioned chair before Bastard's desk, next to the still standing Miguel Evangelista. "What did I miss? How far did you get, girl?"

Bastard realized then what was going on. "Oh shit. It's like that?"

"Yup," M.E. sighed. Coughed. "Pardon me." Bastard poured her a glass of grain. She gulped it down. "Thanks." The drink made NNannette Nonet lighter in air and in voice, but she stayed in character. "M.E. asked me to do it this way. Anyway, now you know." Her Miguel Evangelista eyebrows bled for a refill. Bastard obliged. She concluded, "So yeh – this is a big job, big brother. Tonight, you're breaking into Lance Newcomb's Estate."

Bastard smiled, already in acceptance. Even though he knew that it wasn't M.E. standing before him, he knew that the words spoken in the man's form were truly his, and that his form-fitting friends represented the man's true intention.

"This is on -" he pointed to himself, "?"

"This is all on you, Bastard. M.E. can't do shit, he's in custody."

"Hey yo so – where is this 'custody' you speak of? And what happened to you yesterday – I can tell you what happened to Bastard. I got fucked the fuck up and locked the fuck up. What happened to you two? I know y'all didn't club my head – right?"

"Bastard, we are sorry. Sasia and I wanted to come in here and immediately straight up apologize, but M.E. insisted that we deliver you the message in his image, before making it known that it wasn't him but one of us, so that you wouldn't get distracted with that, so that you would focus entirely on the fact that M.E. is telling you this."

"Makes sense," Bastard conceded.

"Right?" Sasia agreed. "Otherwise I'd've come in with her. I thought it made sense."

"Cool," Bastard was satisfied. "And what is it that I am to steal?"

The two form-fitters looked at each other and

together said, while turning their heads back to face Bastard, "Lance Newcomb's Replenishing Sphere of Flesh Brick."

Bastard smiled at Sasia Stasia and NNannette Nonet, for they were real, and they were lovely friends. One of them leaned over the desk and pushed the dossier closer to Bastard, who understood that the appropriate Time to pick it up had arrived. While he regarded the plans, both of them talked him through the details of the heist.

46

THE DETAILS OF THE HEIST, AS EXPLAINED BY SASIA STASIA AND NNANNETTE NONET.

The first hurdle was the exterior perimeter wall. It had grown to be three men tall and was made of fake stones laid in cement with bits of broken glass splayed (in-/on-)to the surface, not only atop the wall but on the sides as well. To climb over this wall would result in lacerations. Funnily enough, the sharp shards were added to keep people in, not to keep people out.

It is known that Lance Newcomb and Despi'kha Belle had once made a child who, at an early age, was as crazy as a really crazy bat that shits like crazy. By the age of less than one, the kid had escaped from the estate twice. So, Newcomb paid cement peoples to plant shards of broken glass bottles into the wall, to discourage and prevent his son from escaping again.

And it worked. The next time the kid attempted to flee the grounds, he cut himself terribly, and bled to death. Problem solved.

"Next, you will encounter another quadrilateral

boundary," Sasia Stasia picked it up. "It is called deadland, but it is very much alive. And it is here that everything dies. The temperature continues to rise from something already absurdly high to an even higher and more absurd degree.

"The nine-foot stretch of deadland requires the most impervious of skins," it continued. "A desert is comparatively cool and wet. The heat alone is fatal, and when all three sunshines shine, it's even more fatal." The document that Stasia was quoting paused. "The light bakes you, it is too much. It's too hot. And there is no wind, because the air movement from the city's enormous fans don't pass through fake-stone walls (as you know, fake wind only passes through real stone).

"deadland has claimed the lives of all previous burglars, who were all cats – except for the ones that were purported people-ishers like you and M.E. and us. These cats were able to jump over the broken glass-inlaid perimeter wall without cutting themselves. But then they'd land in deadland, and immediately their desiccating corpses were picked apart by chicken vultures before their bones decomposed into dust. (By the way, if you happen to find a purple and yellow cat around there, please bring her home to M.E., who misses the little bastard. My bad."

"No worries. Sounds unlikely, but I've no reason to say no. What's the little fucker's name?"

"Catman."

"Makes sense."

"Not really."

"Okay," Bastard lamented.)

Via Stasia and Nonet, the dossier continued to explicate the mission's initial challenges.

The third ridiculous obstacle was the Rainforests with Beasts. This sounded really dangerous. The Beasts were as big as forty men, some of them (some of the Beasts, not some of the forty men). They could swallow a man whole, especially if they knew how to share. But normally, these carnivorous animals chewed the fuck out of their protein until macerated enough to down like a bloody smoothie.

The weather there was nice, at least, according to everyone who hadn't been. But the shock of the stark contrast in climate and temperature from deadlands to the Rainforests with Beasts shuts down most body's systems. No one has yet been able to enjoy the weather there.

Many different Rainforests with Beasts comprised this region, although they were all connected and undifferentiable. This fact confused Bastard. He decided not to let it bother him.

Then – as if this wasn't already enough – he would have to traverse a stretch of hot coals. The dossier expounded that "The hot coals are VERY hot.

"Most people – those who'd made it that far, which is very few – were set aflame by the radiating red rocks. It is a torturous death, according to those who'd been interviewed. First, the bottom of each foot catches fire, then the soles of both feet waxen into an ooze and become one with the fiery coals. The flames quickly spread up the body, internally and externally. As the extreme heat consumes the body, one suffers the additional horror of smelling one's own burning flesh."

The penultimate obstacle was the Rabid Dog Park. This was a shitfield of rabid canine doo-doo, inhabited by – yup! – rabid dogs. Approximately twenty hundred, although it was hard to keep track with all the deaths from in-fighting and births from in-breeding. But they averaged around this staggering number, the furious drooling sharp-toothed crazy doggies.

And finally, there was nothing. This was supposed to be the greatest challenge, and to overcome it required incredible focus and concentration. The dossier included no information on nothing. It was the last hurdle before the next serious series of impossible tasks, which included getting into the mansion itself, making it to Newcomb's Special Collections, locating the Replenishing Sphere of Flesh Brick, and escaping with it.

"If you pull this off," the two form-fitters spoke in unison, "you'll be able to defeat Lance Newcomb."

"Oh!" exclaimed Bastard. "That would be nice."

Then he had an idea. "Hey, would you help a brother out – I gotta dress right nice for this party I'm off to. I could use some help. And it'll be mad fun, we'll have a good time."

"Can we come to the party? Is it gonna be cool?"

"I would love nothing more than your company, for real for real," Bastard expressed sincerely. "But it's work-related, not fun. In all honesty, I expect it to be an awful party. It's potentially very dangerous, and there's no point in risking all three of our lives for this part. Anyway, I'm going to investigate a White Dove drug den rave, and I don't wanna attract any attention."

They believed Bastard, because he was honest with them. After the party, Bastard would pull off the heist. This made sense, and the three crims agreed that it would be so. Then they spent some time together.

47

NIGHT.

Bastard planned to exit through the back door of his building, wearing a similar disguise to the one he was wearing the other day when he overheard the conversation about tonight's party. Similar, but not the same. He wanted to be recognized, maybe, but not immediately, not completely, not with surety. The idea was to appear no more than familiar.

Sasia Stasia suggested sporting a darker brown fedora than usual, yet lighter than the one he had worn the night before. And instead of a (fake) full beard, NNannette Nonet helped him into a medium-thick Fu Manchu he'd used during his days in the Underground chapter of the Organization's Underground Underground. Everyone from those days was long dead, Bastard recollected, sighing internally. Sussing off the adhesive from the strip of badger-hair whiskers before applying the medium-thick Fu Manchu above his upper lip had brought back many memories of the Cycles he had spent, many moonages ago, during the Second-to-Last-War...

Bastard was going to a party! He donned the green mohair suit that Des had given him before his trip out West...*Des*. He wondered what the fuck she was up to right now...and why she hadn't responded to his last few gropes. Again, he realized that he actually missed her – or at least he felt that way, and he thought that he felt that he felt such longing. But then he wondered why...why, – why – ...why did his brain always return to thinking about Despi?

The heavily starched oversized collar of his shit-brown with urine-yellow striped and bruise-purple dotted suit lay open and rested upon the lapels of his well-fitting jacket (Stasia and Nonet decided against the green mohair suit at the last moment, and changed him in mid-step). His shoes were brand new – they were his favorite and never-previously-worn brown newt leather platform shoes, still moist from the creek where he had found the original efts under a rock, only yesterday, in the Bois de Bleu Loin.

He may not have been dressed that differently, but he appeared a different man. He wasn't Bastard – not at this moment, no. He was just some asshole going to a party.

Bastard exited through the back door of his building in this outfit.

He walked down the street a few steps, then back up a few steps, in order to stay above ground.

The entire population succumbs, he thought to himself. People walk; ground melts; feet depress into the Cube's circular core, leaving dangerous gaping pot-holes for others to fall into. And as the doomed descend deeper into the Cube, the hotter it gets, because this cubular planet is basically a solid fire pit that generates all of the power for the above ground machines that power everything else.

Reportedly, F-E 999 has seized many of these chunnels, milking the generator of its energy for their own purposes – taking over the arteries that previously existed for the good of the people and diverting them to feed their own massive machines.

But the headline that everyone saw that day was "All Energy-Providing Solutions Companies Declare Bankruptcy – Except 'Newbie' F-E 999."

Funny thing was, though, Free-Enterprise 999 wasn't new.

For seven blocks he thought about this shit. Mostly, though, he thought about Des, and all of the ways she could choose to play.

48

COLOR-CODED SCLERA: THE NEWEST LATEST!

The ubiquitous use of the newly introduced "World Enhancer 3000000" produced further challenges to the already confusing practice of social interaction by encouraging people to virtually realize memories and feelings of their own personal fantastical fake-life experiences. It was termed "Bliving," and it was very popular, because it was good and it was true. Many People were walking around in public "Bliving" a separate reality. Not content to disengage with real life, the People could now misengage.

Imagine if someone was experiencing/recalling/ streaming a sad thought/memory/(p)re-memory while walking down the street. And bumped into another person who was "Bliving" winning the Kumite as a kick-boxer. Unwarranted physical aggression is born, altercations would result, and the first person would be badly beaten – even if (s)he were in fact a professional kick-boxer, because (s)he would be caught off guard, in another world, lost in a moment of "Bliving" a vacation with her grandmother who died before (s)he had even been born.

Color-Coded Sclera: The World Enhancer's tinted lenses are pretty self-explanatory:

Red = Angry

Blue = Sad

Green = Balls (greed, avarice, assholism, all that good stuff)

And they'd change colors, every shade of the spectrum in between, to represent different emotions associated with specific experiences/events that didn't necessarily happen.

This new technology had recently been introduced, implemented and disseminated to the entire population, with a threateningly strong official "recommendation" to wear them (according to the Organization's estimates, only seven percent of us were still resisting the mandate).

So everyone that he passed by on the street had crazy colored eyes. Bastard couldn't tell who was looking at what, and people kept bumping into him, which made him shudder nasty giggle-likes...

49

ABOUT THE PARTY WITH THE BLACK SLIME AND A BOAR. BASTARD IS RECAPTURED.

Bastard found the spot. An old factory. He walked up to a large door and pushed it open with some effort.

He was immediately bombarded by excruciatingly loud and shitty music and a horde of morons who did not know that the music was shitty. Perhaps they knew that it was loud – but he couldn't be certain. Overwhelmed and anxious, uncomfortable, Bastard needed a drink.

A bar at the front of the club appeared to greet him. He stole a bottle of grain when the robot wasn't looking and quickly downed half of it. Then he threw the bottle at a speaker hanging from the ceiling. It broke upon impact. Ninety-nine shards of sharp glass rained down on the party-goers, who assumed that this was a deliberately constructed Actuality experience. Even those who were badly slashed and bleeding out of their faces seemed to be digging it, if only suffering for the mis-sake of appearances.

Bastard was barely blending in with the crowd.

The world coughed and he slanted, nearly stumbled. The grids realigned themselves, the squares fell back in place, and the party continued as if nothing had happened. Bastard scoffed at their indifference. "What is this world coming to?" he said to himself, not expecting an answer. One did not arrive. He took in the scene, which was grating at best, before stepping onto the main floor.

Which he immediately regretted doing, as no one was dancing. For some reason, the dance floor was littered with heaps of zombies that hung about in air and space with arms either dangling or flailing.

Bastard wanted to dance, but that wasn't what he had come for. He was pleased to be set back on track by saying to himself, "I am Bastard. I am here to learn more about what this generation is doing with the White Dove, and to see if I can mine some info rocks..."

He looked around while making his way to the back of the enormous warehouse space. His eyes kept returning to the walls. They appeared to be dripping with black slime. The radiating colors of the party lights danced upon the oozing matter that was coming from an invisible place in the ceiling. The source would never be depleted, Bastard somehow knew. He felt an increasing urge to taste the black goo, so he veered towards the left wall.

Bastard stuck out his tongue to scoop up the slime. As soon as he'd made a mouthful, purple stars blew up in his sight behind his eyes, in his brain, bright and shiny and very funny and then dark. Light vibrated inside his mouth as the goop bounced about it and covered his tongue and gums like a pinball of sticky butter that decreased in size until eventually evenly distributed within.

"Blehblehbleh," Bastard said. He used a finger to rub the sludge around and press it in. Suddenly, a very strong restraint seized his shoulder. He turned and looked up at a huge motherfucker in a black suit with a security price tag. He recoiled back and down in horror. He extended his right arm behind him, touched the wall, scooped some muck and quickly licked his fingers – all while maintaining eye contact with the extraordinary freak that towered above and before him.

Swollen gray lips wobbled. Bastard could only assume that the giant was speaking to say something to him. But between the loud music and the effects of the black slime, he understood nothing. He couldn't be sure this thing was even trying to speak to him, because he didn't know whether or not it could speak at all.

They continued to look at each other while Bastard cowered even further in a heightened state of drug-induced paranoia. "Get the fuck away from me! Ach!"

"Wmgheughaljmfguhhahathjatjtrj," the enormous bouncer morphed into an 8-foot wild boar with hairy thick appendages that reached out and grabbed Bastard.

"NO! You do not fucking touch me, sir ape," Bastard explained.

"YYYYYYYYYOOOOOOOOOOUUUUUUUU"""'RRRRR RRRREEEEEEEEE CCCCCCCCCOOOOOOOOOMMMMM MMMMIIIIIIIIIINNNNNNNNNGGGGGGGGG WWWW WWWWWIIIIIIIIITTTTTTTTTTHHHHHHHHHH MMMM MMMMMEEEEEEEEE, FFFFFFFFFUUUUUUUUUCCCC CCCCCKKKKKKKKKKUUUUUUUUUPPPPPPPPP. PPPPPP. PPP.
PPPPPPPPP."

"PPPPPPPPP? ARGH!"

The wild boar lifted Bastard into the air and began storming through the crowd, carrying our hero to the opposite back wall. The beast grunted and grunted. Snot dripped from its snout.

Dangling over the boar's shoulder, Bastard reached out with his left arm and scooped up some more goo from the bleeding black back wall. He licked his fingers and said, "Ahhhhhhhhhhhhhhhhhhhhhh." Then he sneezed, then farted.

Elevator doors appeared before his head; they entered past them. Bastard was dropped to the floor. The floor was black, but it had no black slime. Bastard wanted more black slime!

The doors closed; chains creaked and the small compartment trembled as they began to descend. The walls of the elevator stepped closer and closer in, further with each level down. When they landed at stop, the doors opened.

The fat hog kicked him out of the elevator. Bastard felt like a dead slug stuck to the ground with its own slime. Every futile attempt to pick himself up off the floor only discouraged him more.

He finally gave up trying and into gravity, collapsing limp-muscled face down. He vaguely remembers a sliding sensation, as if something was dragging his body along...

50

CATCH AND RELEASE.

Someone or thing dragged Bastard's body down a long cold dark hallway. He heard some heavy doors open. A few moments later, he was inside what appeared to be a small geodesic domed gray concrete-glass-mirrored room.

"Back so soon, I see?" Bastard heard someone say. He was sure he recognized the voice, and didn't move or look up for fear that he was right. He was equally certain that the question was addressed to him, and that therefore an answer was probably expected of him. "You seem to possess absolutely zero interest in and capacity for self-preservation," the nasally voice continued gratingly. The man's voice was coated in sleaze. Bastard thought he could hear its sweet rank thickness gelling smack smack smack from the meat flapper. "I didn't even pick you up this Time – you actually came to me! Directly here! Are you a fucking idiot??? Oh sorry, I already know that you're an idiot. Hahahahahahaaaa!" It was a very annoying and displeasing laugh; it was fucking up Bastard's high, and he wished it would stop. Unfortunately, the voice kept sounding.

"So," audible signs of movement, "what am I supposed to do with you now, Bastard? Huh? Now, my wife seems to have a soft spot for you – I have no idea why." The guy hadn't waited nearly long enough for Bastard to answer, which Bastard found rude and unfair. "I see no redeeming characteristics in your person, nor any value whatsoever in your pathetic life...perhaps it is because you are so helpless and vulnerable, weak and stupid, that she is instinctually attracted to you – whereas that characteristic inspires me to make you suffer even more."

"Can you please shut the fuck up, man? My head is splitting..."

"Ah yes, an unfortunate side effect of the black slime, yes. Apologies – not to you. The kids don't seem to care, as long as they have enough strong analgesics to curb that pain. And most of them are all high on the White Dove, so they don't give a shit.

"Anyway, I must say, Bastard, that your little operation has surpassed my expectations, which were admittedly not very high. But the White Dove is a great drug, naturally. And just because one of yours discovered it doesn't mean you deserve my respect."

"What the fuck, man," Bastard rolled over onto his stomach and started slowly pushing himself up off the floor. "What do you want? Why do you keep trying to take my ass out the game? Where is M.E.???"

"To answer your questions in reverse order: I have your precious partner, Evangelista, in my custody. Don't worry – M.E. is safe, until tomorrow. I will be escorting him personally to the courthouse, where your friend will be tried, sentenced immediately, and summarily executed. I can't wait to see that. And I want you to see it, too."

Climbing up from the ground, Bastard doled himself out onto a chair. He straightened his back and neck, took a deep breath, and looked into Newcomb's dastardly eyes. Bastard said nothing.

"Now, as to why I keep trying to take your ass out of the game..." Newcomb queased. "I guess you are dumb as fuck, so I shouldn't be surprised that you need me to explain."

Bastard was still putting himself together, gathering his thoughts. He waited for Newcomb to continue his nauseating speech.

"Okay, well. It's not that I can't afford to have some competition in the drug trade – I might even welcome it! Could be fun, ya know. With rival gangs and shit. Our goons could exchange showers of bullets in turf battles while our guns clap on the sidelines above their heads... But that's not going to happen – and not because you haven't even entered the competition! Haha! There are too many reasons, honestly. It's complicated. But the most important reason is that you are doing something illegal."

"What the fuck are you talking about??? No shit what we do is illegal. Tha fuck you care? You just said that our operation isn't fucking with you and your enterprises. And even if it did, you're the richest man in history, you don't need more...riches. If you spent a gazillion balls a day, you would still be a multi-bazillionaire when you finally die – even if it's true that you may never will... You're a fucking – "

"Bastard, shush. You're missing the point. I'm not saying that what you're doing is illegal, and that is the problem. I get away with it all the fucking time, every .

single day. The problem is that you are doing something, and that is illegal. I have – "

"You have connections, I know, asshole. You're from an old royal family, and you're probably also the Grand Vampire, and you really fucking scare the shit out of me, because I'm afraid of pain and death and you represent those very scary states of being, if you will, not only symbolically but also behaviorally and verbally as you continue to try to kill me. So yeh, I cower in fear at your superior presence." Bastard coughed. "Oh, and I forgot. I don't care. Fuck you."

"Shut up for a minute, Bastard. I have Old Privilege. You do not. I have permission from the Magistrates to do business here in the Nation. You do not. In fact, the Magistrates *asked* me to do this – I initially refused, having never had an interest in chemistry. But I've developed quite a fondness for 'the game,' as you crims like to say. I'm even getting into the lingo, see! Your culture seems to place little value on the individual, on individual lives, and I dig the callous colloquialisms of a business that enslaves and sickens and kills for profit. Which is ultimately why I couldn't justify any moral defense against operating a Licensed Pharmaceutical Distribution Center.

"Anyway, I wanted to kill you because you're causing trouble, you've always caused trouble, you're a deviant derelict and a disrespectful delinquent doper detective who is disliked by the democracy of the dictating dynasty. The Magistrates asked me to get rid of you, Bastard, and M.E.. So that's what I'm doing. Additionally, I've grown to dislike you, personally, which makes the work enjoyable. Despi'kha is a great player in this, by the way – and this has become my game, now, and trust me, she's playing with my balls, by my rules.

"And what do I want from you, right? That was your first question, in case you don't remember. Well, it's an interesting question, because the answer to that seems to be constantly changing. Right now, all you need to know is that I no longer wish you dead. No... No, I want you alive, at least for the Time being. Exactly why, I cannot tell you. Maybe I already did, actually. I'll remind you – after you have served your purpose. Then, I will kill you or have you killed, finally – depending on my schedule. For now, however, we must postpone your execution.

"Lastly,"

"You gotta be kidding me, man!!! You've been talking through the last several paragraphs, give me fucking break," Bastard irritatedly intoned.

"Lastly," Newcomb loudly projected, "tell me, Bastard: where is Des right now?"

Bastard exhibited his surprise. "You mean, you don't know?"

"No, I don't know, clearly. If I knew where she is, I would not have asked you, 'Where is Des?' Makes sense? How daft are you? Unbelievable."

"You are a very unpleasant man, asshole."

"I have no interest, Bastard, in 'pleasing' anyone – least of all you. Nor do I have Time for unproductive chit-chat. This dialogue has gone on too long, and it's advanced nothing. I'm losing my patience here – it's a simple fucking question, but I'll repeat it for you, in sympathy for your mental deficiencies. Where is my wife?"

Bastard considered the implications of what Newcomb had just revealed. He couldn't be sure, though, what it meant, because there were too many possibilities. He'd have to tease it out of the old man.

Pretending to have dropped something on the floor,

Bastard bent over in his chair and made to look under the desk. "If we look together, dipshit, maybe we can find your patience..."

"That is neither clever nor amusing. You – "

"Yeah okay, stop talking already. A dialogue requires more than one person talking. So listen. I'll tell you straight: the last Time I fucked your wife was a couple nights ago. Honestly, I didn't think you cared."

"It's none of your goddamned business whether or not I care. We've been married for hundreds of hundreds of Large Cycles. She always comes back to me – always. If I cared about you, I might consider it unfortunate that you fell so hard for her. She was never to be available to you. It was a con. And you're just another sucker on the vine." Lance's face had been getting tighter and knottier and bigger and redder, his voice loudening and intensifying.

"So you haven't seen her, either?" Bastard tried to use a more sympathetic tone of voice in an attempt at considerate commiseration.

"Get the fuck out of here before I change my mind and decide to kill you now."

51

BASTARD GOES HOME AND REVIEWS THE DOSSIER ON THE HEIST. AS AGREED, NOW IS THE BEST TIME TO PULL IT OFF.

The Clock said, "It's Time to leave."

Bastard said, "Cool."

He got his shit together and headed out. It was a lot of shit, and he carried it in a large black duffel bag.

Street level on the street, he headed to the Underground Railroad. Six blocks walk. Down the stairs. Uptown.

Wait.

When the train comes, get on the train.

Lance Newcomb's Estate was in another party of the City. Uptown, of course. It should take him two-thirds of one Circle to get there. Bastard spent the time reviewing the plan in his headspace. Seemed simple enough. Then he dreamt about galleries of oddities history artifacts and aliens, showcased in rooms of plush dark red velvet.

He   nearly   missed   the   stop.   He   exited   the

Underground Railroad cart and walked up the dark cold cement steps to the surface land of the unfamiliar neighborhood. Then he walked in the right direction until he found the perimeter of the Lance Newcomb Estate, where he was prepared to face a series of six obstacles.

52

THE HEIST, INCLUDING THE SIX OBSTACLES OF THE LANSION'S EXPANSE.

Bastard figured that the most obvious way to overcome the first obstacle would be the best. And so, he had brought with him a large and very thick gooey rubber mat thingy to cover the wall from the ground to the ground.

He hoped that the blanket would prove thick enough to cover and absorb, so to speak, the large shards of glass. Fortunately, as you will be told soon, it did prove thick enough.

Bastard pulled the enormous blanket out of his bag. With an accompanying groan, he barely managed to hoist it over the wall. It was heavier than a gross gaggle of geese in a large and heavy safe.

The blanket proved thick enough, as you already know, for his corpse mass to overmake. He landed mostly on the bottom of his feet and with barely enough Time to look up and say, "Fuck, man. Pretty sure I would have pulled several muscles, popped out a kneecap, and slipped some discs, had I still a properly functioning body."

A large sigh of relief exuded from his form like a tire releasing pressure, if the tire did so from many tiny holes yet with dignity and control.

As Bastard thought about the pain he would have sustained, he stabled his eyes and assessed his position. There was no life of any kind to be seen. Just light and sandshine and future pain and cutting slicing hot white light heat.

Even the sand seemed to be dying.

To conquer The deadland, he had packed a special jacket that made him look like a fourth sun. This way, the real three would confuse him for one of their own, and not bother him as much. Moreover, the hot sands would shy away and bury themselves, as they had to, in deference to the suns. The special jacket would shield him from the harsh environment. It was green.

He walked for what seemed like much longer than he actually did. It is amazing, he thought to himself as he traversed the desert terrain, That even at night, all three suns shine here. Bastard attributed this to a cryptic concord between Newcomb and the Sun Gods, which is the government agency that holds the suns accountable. (The three suns had lost consciousness, and were not aware that there shouldn't be a fourth, for they're not four but three. His was a clever ruse. Newcomb had had the Magistrates turn a blind eye. Yes. They all had one eye.)

A sudden and drastic change in temperature, humidity, and environment signaled that he'd entered a completely different ecosystem. The various temperaturial degrees, in conjunction with other observable apparencies, forced Bastard to logically and correctly conclude that he was now in the Rainforests with Beasts.

Beyond the initial greens and browns and wets that greeted him, he sensed the presence of great dangers. And when the hordes of hungry hippos picked up Bastard's scent, he heard them begin to howl in organized confusion. The scary sounds encouraged him to move quickly. He rapidly shed his sun-suit and pulled out (and on) his next costume: the not inappropriately named outfit called The Beast.

This was a beautiful instrument of death. Would there be an art of one thousand percent decimation, The Beast would be the whole movement's masterpiece of destruction work. The various tones that one could achieve from playing it depend enteerily on what you're aiming at, ultimately.

How he had fit this (and each and all other) thing(-s) into his bag will forever remain a mystery – until someone solves it. The instrument measured some length, and it made many different sounds including sputtering, hissing, banging, ch-chonging! and bla-blaugh-de-ding!. And they all individually expressed themselves.

Within and at the end of its range was a bowie knife-like bayonet. Bastard utilized this to advance in position, waving The Beast around, chopping things down, forging his way. He was very careful not hurt the vaguely living trees, doing his best to whack only their bionic limbs.

An old saying – something like, "When a forest crumbles, if someone sees it, does the tree know?" occurred to Bastard. This memorably confusing question caused him great anxiety. He wondered if the beasts within the Rainforests with Beasts ever worried about it. In the event of the total devastation of their habitat, what would they do? Who would know, if not the trees?

The herds were able to sense that Bastard considered their plight, and his compassion rendered the Beasts useless – as in no longer useful in performing their purpose of protecting the Estate from intruders. For the Beasts sensationalized his empathy and let him pass. As he strode past the slobbering sniveling creatures, he saw some of them smile. They made so many weird honking oinks and growls – each of which would have to be spelled differently.

Bastard realized that he didn't need to wear The Beast, and decided to make a peace offering of it to the beasts that inhabited the Rainforests with Beasts. Their grunts were clearly in appreciation of his gesture. Bastard laid the article of death down upon the land. The pack of monsters proceeded to ravage it with their teeth and claws and other parts of their bodies that assisted them in dismantling the weapon. Then they dug a large hole in the ground and buried the busted biscuit, after which they looked at Bastard. He understood their head nods to mean that he was allowed to pass through to the next territory. According to the plans, this would be the Very Hot Coals part.

Having relinquished The Beast, his pack was now much lighter, for which he was accidentally grateful. The lesser load would help him move more quickly over the coals. But he wasn't too worried, for he had worn some really special shoes. All he had to do was press his left nipple, and the soles of the shoes would rise, elevating him to about five straightened Circles above the Rose!

These shoes were designed by Haile Leburik and gifted to M.E. by the Abbott, who commissioned the project. The recipe for the soles required the Abbott's personally genetically modified yeast, for which he wished to find new applications. Miguel Evangelista never once wore the shoes, so they were basically brand-new hand-me-downs.

The heat of the coals assisted in the rising of Bastard's soles. However, the temperature of the fiery floor was set too high, and Bastard began to smell his shoe-bottoms burning as he progressed in his airy dance across the flaming furnace. The excessive heat simultaneously worked for and against Leburik's designer shoes. When Bastard approached the halfway point, the Abbott's yeast's functionality potential had reached its peak, and he began to descend from the lofty air nigh the Rose. With each step forward, he got logarithmically closer and closer to the ground.

He picked up the pace, barely making it to the Rabid Dog Park before the Very Hot Coals consumed what was left of that which prevented contact between the bottom of both fleshy feet and what they physically and gravitationally depended upon.

As he had drunk quite a bit before leaving the office, Bastard suddenly had to pee. With contempt, he was doubly relieved to direct the distribution of his urination upon as many of the hot rocks that his stream could touch. This departure was in stark contrast with his surpassing the Rainforests with Beasts, which was amicable, and he thought about this.

But not for long. The rabid dogs had noticed his trespass. They seemed very hungry. Again, Bastard referred to the dossier in his mind. As the barking intensified, he set down his sack to grab the next thing he needed to get through this combat arena.

He walked towards the rabid dogs with arms outstretched, carrying in his hands an impressive selection of spoiled rotting meats, which he tossed at their teeth. Empty-handed, he was able to approach the dogs and pet them. "It is not your fault that you are here," Bastard said.

The dogs must have picked up on the fact that Bastard also had rabies, for they wagged their tails in compatriotism. M.E. must have forgotten that Bastard had rabies. It was not mentioned in the plans. This condition proved helpful.

nothing followed the Rabid Dog Park. And no one had ever made it this far. Bastard knew this, because – according to the dossier – no one had ever reached the Rainforests with Beasts. Again, he wondered how all of this information had been acquired and compiled.

Bastard had prepared himself for the worst for nothing. But it wasn't so bad. It reminded him of being dead. He walked straight up to the house, where a man was standing.

53

BASTARD ENTERS LANCE NEWCOMB'S ESTATE. (TO BE CONTINUED...).

Bastard was not surprised at the sight of some physical presence, undoubtedly stationed to prevent outsiders from passing through the palace's portal.

As he approached, he regarded the man who guarded the entry with a gat. Funny – he was pretty sure he knew this cat. Even though he couldn't totally recall (at all) how he knew the motherfucker, he sensed that he was his illk. Then, the guy's eyes convinced him that he oughtta recognize.

"What's up, man?" Bastard suggested.

"Ohhh shit!!! Bastard!" the dude exclaimed with genuine enthusiasm.

Oh shit, Bastard thought. He knows my name. I don't remember his name.

"Man, it's good to see you." Bastard looked to his left and right, scoping out the garden, checking the facade of Lance's personal living-building.

Breathing, he scored the heavy's face. His eyebrows

were of medium-hairy length, and irregularly patched in certain spots with lighter colored, newer flesh. His face was adorned with other old scars. When Bastard clocked the identifying half-buck-fifty on the left side of the face, he suddenly recollected something(s). They used to call him Seventy-Five Cents. But he still couldn't remember the dude's name.

Bastard smiled, because he knew fondness for this guy. "When did you get out, man? And what are you doing, workin' for this twatsack?"

"What?" he laughed, "tha fuck you doin' alive? When I got out, I heard you were dead. And what are you doing, here?"

"Long story. And yes, I did. And again, long story," Bastard answered in respective succession. "Dude, can I go in there – the house, I mean?" he said, pointing at the house.

"Of course you can. What's goin' on?"

"Well, I'm here to steal Newcomb's Replenishing Sphere of Flesh Brick," he explained. "I don't wanna get you in trouble with work, though."

"Fuck it. Lance Newcomb's an asshole. Did you know that he actually named his mansion the Lansion? That's fucking stupid," Man guffawed. "Anyway, you cool. I was planning on quittin' soon, for real. So I'm,a just walk away from this. Do your thing, Bastard."

"Wait, man. Say, are there any malintentioned beings inside?"

"Nope! I'm the only one here, Bastard. No one's ever gotten this far – passed past the six obstacles. So there's little need for security at the house. Unless Newcomb has guests, which is never, because he's an evil asstard and has no friends. I've always felt my job here was redundant. Hence my no-longer-forthcoming resignation."

"Thanks, Man," Bastard recovered. His forgetfulness would go unnoticed. "Much appreciated."

"No worries, happy to help an old mate. And the Organization. Much love, Bastard, much respect. If you need anything, get at your boy. You know I got you."

"Likewise. You already know. That's how we do."

They embraced.

He watched Man walk to a black car that was parked nearby in the circle driveway, get in it, and drive away. Once inside the strange house, Bastard felt unHeimlichly comfortable. He closed the door behind him.

54

CONT'D: IN ORDER TO STEAL SOMETHING
IMPORTANT FOR A GOOD REASON.

The foyer opened up to a large high-ceilinged space with walls. There were rooms to the left and right, and more rooms beyond the dual staircase before him. He would have loved to explore, but he had a mission.

After much deliberation, he chose the left staircase. The second level was all and entirely water. Walking up the stairs, the first thing to get wet was the top of his head. When he had reached the top of the landing, he was fully immersed in water.

It was easy for him to swim up to the third floor, because he was a good swimmer, and he would have floated up anyway. But why this group of water would choose to obey certain laws of physics and yet defy others, Bastard could not fathom. I wondered about this, too.

He stepped out of the floating pool, onto the floor of the third floor. None of this made sense – but on second thought, it did. Anyone who couldn't swim, or was allergic to water, would never get this high.

Because Bastard had swum to the surface so quickly, his clothes weren't completely soaked through. Grateful, he followed the signs for the Special Collections.

It is difficult to resist the temptation to detail all of the wonders that Lance Newcomb held in his household. However, it is even harder to explain. In later editions, there could be an addendum, perhaps with a map.

Bastard had no idea what a Replenishing Sphere of Flesh Brick looked like. But he was right in assuming that he would know when he found it. On a raised pedestal of silver and purple and blue and other colors that have names and others that remain unnamed, nestled in a nest of nets, an anti-shape glowed like the tissue of a yellow-orange pulsating brain, interiorly illuminated.

He kneeled down to pull a pair of gloves from his pack. Bastard was warned that any tactile contact with the Flesh Brick would make his sphere forever replenish – a condition now known as refleshing – and he would become immortal. For the possession of the power of the Replenishing Sphere is transferable, and belongs solely to the One who has touched it last. But if he wore these special kind of gloves, he could pick it up.

He placed the Replenishing Sphere of Flesh Brick inside a paper bag. Even though the weird muscle mass appeared to be dry, the paper bag got wet. He was going to remove it and place it within a plastic bag, but he knew that the Replenishing Sphere of Flesh Brick needed to be able to breathe. So instead, he took off his pants and carefully wrapped the pair around the miraculous anti-geometric treasure. He gently placed the package within his duffel bag, making sure that the thing could breathe, and settling it in a position similar to that in its previous bed.

Leaving the sack open for air, Bastard picked it up and started walking towards the Elevator sign. Then he followed a directional arrow, and arrived at an elevator. He pressed the "Summon" button and something dinged and the doors opened and he got on the platform and pressed the button for the "Rooftop + Helipad." The doors closed, and as the device ascended, Bastard remarked upon the fact that there was a "2" button for the "Second Floor."

"How does that work?" he wanted to know. But he would never find out, because he didn't have enough Time to try it, go back down, see what would happen. His helicopter was already there, waiting for him, ready to go. Bastard ran towards, got in, and the chopper lifted. Into the air.

XERXES (ELEVEN)

55

THE TIME HAS COME TODAY.

The next morning, Bastard woke up feeling great. This struck him as odd, for it was unusual.

When the phone call rang, he answered it. "Yeah, come over," he hung up the phone.

This Xerxes was the Final Day of the Absolute Conditional Beneficial Judiciary Hearing of the Kingdom of the Nation VS. Newt Humbert in the Trial of the Guns and Butter Case. It was a momentous day, and its arrival meant the departure of Miguel Evangelista the following day. Although Bastard had not seen M.E. for several Circles, it was nice to know that he was around. He knew that he would miss his dear friend, and so he wept.

Bastard lit up a spliff and proceeded to prepare for the party. He donned his best suit, because his other ones were dirty. This one was a beautiful horse brown hair suit cut in the ficticio-historical style of the Second Ancient Romans. With a hysterical dark blue ocean (liquid) shirt, with matching socks and handkerchief of larvae-shit silk. Brown fedora to match, elephant-spit shined constrictor leather shoes.

Bastard thought he looked fucking sharp, but he needed to know. He sharpened his ocular focus on his reflection upon the surface of a recently discovered mirror that hung on one of his office room's four walls (not the wall with the door to the waiting room that no one used, nor the one with the door to his bedroom). And he did look good to himself – but he wanted to know how he might appear to other people. So he took down the mirror and placed it in the bottom left corner of the wall. From his bedroom he brought another mirror, and set this one in the same corner, but against the other wall, so that the two mirrors would meet at an edge of the cube.

Regarding himself thusly, Bastard was satisfied that others could see that he looked fucking sharp and said, "Word." Then he re-placed both mirrors, and took a familiar seat behind his desk.

Bastard's buzzer buzzed.

He pressed a button under his desk and the doors to his office would have opened had they not already been in splinters on the floor, knocked down by The sloth. Bastard didn't know who had removed the dead body, nor did he know why, or how, or when, or what. He decided that he didn't need to know, and was grateful that it was so.

Having no need to open doors, in walked Sasia Stasia and NNannette Nonet, each carrying a suitcase and a duffel bag, as well as other various-sized functional accessories.

"Thanks," Bastard smiled. "Let's go in there," nodding at the wall that separated his office from the bedroom. They knew what was there from previous visits, and led the way through. Bastard followed. Sasia and NNannette threw their bags on the bed and opened them up to reveal a cache of small arms and artillery.

"Fucking hell," Bastard mused, amused. "Damn." He took his hands off his hips and approached the portable armory. "And this is all Officially Approved Stamped?"

"Yup," said NNannette.

"We stole all this shit from the fucking precinct, so yeah, Bastard! And it's a lot of beautiful fucking shit, if I may say so myself."

"Well, you may. You're the experts! So tell us, what do we need?"

"All right," Sasia maintained. "You need to be able to carry this shit into the Courts, that's what you were saying? You're goin' to the Date, right?"

"Yeh. But we're all going to the Date."

"Aha! Okay that's great, because we can carry more shit amongst the three of us."

"Exactly, my friends. You two're the best. Now, what we got here."

NNannette picked up a small brown piece and handed it to Bastard.

"Not only do you need this, but it matches your outfit. You look good, bwoi."

"I know!" Bastard exclaimed, happy.

They both laughed at him. "Feel that shit: – it's light, right?"

"Light as fuck."

"Pop the clip."

He did. "Fuck."

"Yeh," Sasia resumed. "Exactly. That clip fits two dozen hairline fracture bullets – you see that tiny sliver of – pull out one of the bullets – hold it up to the light – you see that tiny sliver of green shining through the casing?"

"Yeah, shit."

"That's immediate death."

"In a hairline fracture bullet??? How'd you get it in there?"

"I didn't. Neither did she. We can't explain it, I'm sorry. Just know it is there, and use it."

"Thank you, my friends."

"Sure, baby. Now here's another one – same exact piece. They'll fit in your fucking pocket, put 'em in your pants, one on each side. It's like it ain't even there."

"Wow. Okay. What's next?"

"Take this." NNannette handed him a miniature cellephonic device, gave one to Sasia, and kept one herself.

"You know I – "

"Yeh, shut the fuck up. I'm not gonna call you, Bastard. Put that thing in the front right side pocket of your jacket." He complied.

"Now take these," Sasia spoke, handing him a bunch of black beads on a string. "Put these rosaries in your other front jacket pocket, left side."

He obeyed, but started fingering the big beads and she snapped, "Dude, don't play with them, please. They're incredible incredibly tiny bombs."

"Ooh!"

"If you wanna get a bunch of assholes at once, bowl these on the ground. They'll all roll down together and stretch out like a snake and encircle your target. You can take out a clustered group like that. Or you can hold and release one end, and all the little bead bombs will come off the string and go all over the fucking place. Soon as people start thinking that you've simply lost your marbles, you press the top button on that phone I just gave you, and they'll all explode. Each single spherical shell contains one cc of hydronitroglycerin."

"Thanks."

"Don't mention it. Here," Sasia handed him a long black tube-like thing. Then some Velcro. "Here, strap that piece to your leg."

Bastard lifted his right pants leg up and taped the pipe against the side of his shin.

"It's not a pipe. It's a fucking blowtorch-dart gun. So simple to use, to explain it to you would be insulting. You fucking blow into it. Fireball-darts come out. People get hit with them, if you can aim."

"Cool, cool. We got any grenades?"

"Bwoi!" she laughed.

"Son! I thought you'd never ask!" NNannette handed him six medium grenades from another bag on the bed. She looked at him. "Take off your jacket."

"Do we have time for this?" he asked as he followed her instructions.

She ignored the question, handed him a small roped-sack and said, "Here, put your arms through these loops, and hang this part around your neck, so the pouch rests on your tummy. Tuck the grenades in there, and put your jacket back on. Every Time you breathe, you'll remember that you have this choice."

Bastard was so pleased. His face hurt from smiling. "Hey, why do you keep telling your boy where to put everything?"

"Ha!" NNannette scoffed.

Sasia explained like to a child, "This way, you'll know where everything is, Bastard."

"Ha-HA! Very smart. What's next?"

The three compatriots spent the greater part of another Circle and a half divvying up the arsenal, until they had packed as much as they could carry.

56

IN WHICH BASTARD, SASIA STASIA, AND NNANNETTE NONET ROLL UP.

He felt a bit heavy with all the equipment he was carrying, but the extra weight also made him more confident. The first thing that Bastard noticed when he walked into the courtroom was the presence of the Jokerman Infidel, who was seated in the back of the houseroom. His funny green hat, Bastard saw it from behind. And as if the little freak had sensed Bastard's fresh presence, he turned his head around and flashed his wicked green grin. Bastard offered a malicious smile to the little devil in return.

Fuck, he thought to himself. Fuck fuck fuck. He scanned the room, which was populated by people. Those who had something to do with the procedure stood or sat up front; those that had less to do with it sat further back.

He returned his eyes to where the Jokerman Infidel had been sitting, but was no longer. The sly fellow had reseated himself closer to the action, in the middle of the room, to the right.

Bastard took a seat in the last row, as planned.

"All rise," a little man in the front shouted a bit too aggressively, "for the Presiding Residing Most Revered Reverend Honorable Justice Lance Newcomb, Judge, Jury, and Executioner."

57

OH FUCK.

Oh fuck, Bastard thought to himself, again. This probably isn't going to go as well as expected, he grumbled internally. Good thing I brought the cavalry...

Sasia and NNannette had taken their assigned seats up in the front row, at opposite ends.

"Be seated, or remain standing," Newcomb boomed. "I will sit down."

There was murmuring in the courtroom because that's what people do in courtrooms when they sit down.

Newcomb began the hearing with no introduction. "State your name?"

"Miguel Evangelista. You know that."

"Just answer the questions. Do you understand the charges against you?"

"Nope! I do not beg your pardon, but I'm not here to be tried, man. I'm here as an I-witnessed, in defense of the Kingdom of the Nation, against Newt Humbert."

"Uh-huh. I agree with you that you likely believe this

is the case. But do you really think the Magistrates would allow you back in the Nation to testify against an invented defendant – in a case in which you are implicitly complicit?"

"This is duplicitous!" M.E. reprimanded the ruler.

58

BASTARD DECIDES THAT NOW IS THE TIME
(OR, TALK - ACTION = SHIT).

Miguel Evangelista was standing before him in shackles, chained from his bruised and tender and bleeding wrists and ankles to concrete blocks within the witness chair. His hair was greasy, unclean, and unkempt; his skin lighter, ashen; his eyes duller; he seemed to have gained weight, but at the same time looked skinnier. But he stood tall, solemnly yet confidently, as if he already knew that he had been finally defeated – and also knew, with the most profound of personal conviction, that he was right, that he was in the right, that he had been right, that he had right on his side and his back and his front. Any judgment made in this courtroom, whatever might occur in this space and whatever this charade resulted in – none of it mattered to M.E..

As the court proceeded with its accusations, Bastard felt comforted by the Truth. For, in accord with the rules of the Organization, Bastard and M.E. did not believe in the laws of the Nation. They did not value, or abide by, another group's irrational rules, imposed on submissive subjects of a paternalistic totalitarian capitalist oppressive fascist plutocracy. They did not respect its judicial system, and did not believe in the courtroom in which one of their own was currently standing trial – and therefore Bastard knew that nothing that had happened or was happening or would happen in this here space mattered. Because all of the elements that constituted and made up his present experience – what anyone else would consider to be one's actual environment and one's place within it – none of them were real.

Bastard quietly pulled the rosaries from his pocket and cut the ends of the strings, releasing the spherical explosives with motivational force from his hand. The little bombs rolled silently across the floor of the courtroom and stopped at the feet of the seat of Lance Newcomb and the wall of security officers elsewhere up front.

Sasia Stasia and NNannette Nonet stood up when Bastard did. They maintained their positions, now with their biscuits precisely pointed at Newcomb's big bald shiny head, as Bastard approached the bench.

"Be seated," Lance Newcomb pronounced in his powerful alto.

Bastard looked at Evangelista, and then at Stasia and Nonet. Everyone nodded.

"Fuck you, you hateful dying piece of shit," Bastard announced. He reached into his right front suit jacket pocket, wherein he pressed a designated button on a certain item. POPOP.OPOPOPOPOOPOPOPOPOPOOOP POPOOOOPPOOOP.POPOPOPOPOPOPOPOPOPOPOP OPO.PPOOOOPP, all of the bangs of the ball-like bead bombs sang.

Some people died while others screamed. An

extraordinary amount of Circles seemed to pass as Bastard progressed halfway up the aisle towards his friend and his enemy. His perception of Chronometry and Air Shape twisted, expanding and deepening and slowing down around him. A dissociating hollow ring had moved in and taken up residence in his ears, muffling and distantiating the current sounds in the room in favor of previous sounds, like a dying man being suffocated with a pillow. Far away, he heard a woman stifling tears of fear, sniffling hysterically but quietly. He heard Lance Newcomb trying to breathe normally, sucking at desperate gasps, pretending to grasp composure and control. The last of the bodyguard-cops shuddered a final and strained, pathetic breath, before relaxing into the floor, expired.

Bastard reached for the Replenishing Sphere of Flesh Brick as he continued to walk through the smoke and settling debris. Somehow, he exited his body. His consciousness arose from out of his physical form and floated up to the ceiling of the courtroom, from where Bastard observed his corporeal vessel. The motion stopped, like a still of a scene in which no one knows they're being shot.

By this point, his actual grounded body had nearly reached the front of the courtroom. Miguel Evangelista and Lance Newcomb seemed frozen in form in place, fixated as the violence and uncertainty commanded the air before them. And while his mind was still up in the air, an impulse carried his outer head to turn and clock the top of the inner circle of the cube. And up in the right corner of the ceiling near the entrance to the courtroom hovered the Jokerman Infidel, poised with a double-barrel shotgun that he aimed directly at Bastard's physical head.

Bastard immediately returned to his body and yelled

at himself, "Drop to the ground – get out the fuckin' way, Bastard!"

He sent his mass awkwardly yet stealthily down and to the left, avoiding the bullet's trajectory. His ribs hit the floor first. He scattled to the side, to the safety of the shield of the pews, shocking himself with a sudden flourish of some innate, animalistic sense of self-preservation. And then he heard the pull of the trigger and the clap of the gun.

59

THIS IS THE END.

When he looked up, he saw his friend's body react to the violent absorption of a small foreign object. Bastard had evaded the bullet, but the bullet had proceeded to hit M.E..

As Miguel Evangelista physically processed the projectile, he looked at me and I met his eyes. I could feel his dark trenchant peepers take hold of mine, and my body seized at the moment that a second bullet met my friend's chest, piercing his skin and puncturing his heart. His body jerked back at first, as far as the shackles permitted, before it whipped back upright; M.E. shuffled his shoes in a struggle to stay standing.

I stared at him, unable to move or speak or breathe, while he returned my gaze with intense ferocity and urgency. I submitted and accepted, and suddenly he began communicating everything to me: he was transferring his vast wealth of knowledge and experience, his life energy and his mental database, to me – so that I would know everything that he knew, and his consciousness could enter into my own.

In his final moments, M.E. told me everything; he taught me all that he had yet to confer upon me, and sent me all of his ammaterial possessions. He gave me his naked soul, and I received his curious, criminal genius.

He then raised his gaze above and beyond me. I could sense his spirit withdrawing; I knew that he was looking at his assassin. So as I watched my dearest friend begin to whither and disappear, I jumped back up and spun around, Glock drawn, aiming in the direction that felt right, recalling an image from a memory of just before...

I emptied the full clip before even opening his eyes. Five of the six shots Bastard had fired made contact. The small body of the funny-looking bounty hunter suddenly dropped from its place on the ceiling and landed atop a pew. The impact produced a surprisingly loud "SNAP" as his bones broke and his body folded in half, limp and lifeless.

I turned around and contacted eyes with NNannette Nonet and then Sasia Stasia, who still had their guns steadily trained at Newcomb's bulbous brain-frame. They barely nodded, and discharged their pieces. The independent series of bullets burrowed two perfect, tiny tunnels through the Grand Vampire's dome piece, criss-crossing each other's path, creating an Xpattern cHannell, four little holes mathematically spaced around the circumference of the head.

Because Bastard had bagged the Replenishing Sphere of Flesh Brick, Lance Newcomb was no longer immortal. And it was thus that he could be killed, and for why he then died.

Without the spherical brick's replenishment of flesh freshing, Newcomb's neurological activity ceased at the introduction of the bullets to his brain. The evil genius behind Free-Enterprise 999 was dead.

Oddly, though, Bastard felt frustrated, as if Newcomb's death affirmed his own life. For a split second circle, Bastard considered the absolute futility of everything, the meaninglessness of it all. Then he reflected on the object for immortality – and he realized that it was the way to his death.

As Newcomb's body slumped lifeless in that throne of a judge's seat, Bastard couldn't help but release an uncomfortable and heartfelt laugh. Newcomb's misrepresentationally impressive, domineering stature had crumbled so quickly that it was difficult to reconcile the resulting weak sack of skin and bones as having once constituted the most powerful and ruthless and evil of men-things.

Bastard's mind returned to his dead friend, and he briefly mourned the departure of this extraordinary, beautiful, brilliant and hilariously subversive revolutionary being. Miguel Evangelista's body lay sprawled on the floor behind the pulpit; Bastard could not see his friend for the obstruction, and yet he knew that M.E. was still there.

All of this had occurred within the span of a very small Circle.

60

WHY?

Bastard looked at Sasia and NNannette, wordlessly signaling to them that the time had come to vacate the premises...

Their return eyes asked compassionately what they should do with Miguel Evangelista's body. Should they take it with them, honor him by burying it with respect?

Bastard shook his head, "No. For his body is now an empty shell. It no longer houses the man that we loved so dearly. It does not matter at all what happens to a previously animated, now inert physical mass. Miguel would have preferred us not to waste our Time on such inane trivialities. He's fucking dead, but if he wasn't, he'd be screaming at us to get the fuck out of this crime scene place as soon as fucking possible."

Sasia and NNannette fell in line behind Bastard, and they proceeded together past the rows of rows until they reached the front entrance, which was now the front exit.

They turned left out the door and walked down the

hallway towards the elevator. Nobody said a word – neither did any of them. One little circle later, the lift arrived. Its brash notifying "DING" – although expected – startled the three of them. That sound...it seemed such a jarring offense. It understood nothing, it had no awareness, no consciousness of anything that had just taken place, of anything that had taken place in the past, of anything that would take place. And it would continue to make such noises and go up and down regardless of what happened to anyone and everyone and everything, until it no longer did. Its basic functioning would persist through all, until it eventually broke down or the Nation was bombed or everything was gone.

Bastard still had his gun drawn. When the elevator doors opened and several anti-peace officers startled forth – Deputies of the National Order of Civil Stability and the Execution of the Upholdment of National Law – he summarily popped one bullet into each of the seven soldiers of civil war.

Sasia and NNannette acted fast and dragged the dead bodies out of the elevator and into the hallway.

They entered the lift. Someone pressed the button for the ground floor. Bastard leaned, exhausted, against the back wall of the small, enclosed vessel. The moving box descended.

"Are you okay?" Sasia asked him, softly, worriedly, with the kind of sweetness that comes only with salt.

"I am fine," he finally spoke.

He sighed. "Yeh. Yeh, I'm fine." He softly sounded these empty words without confidence, considering that he knew not what awaited him next, what he would be presented with in his immediate and not so immediate future, what struggles and tortures and pain and despair – what joys, what loves, what pleasures – he had yet to experience, what adversities he would have to face, and may have to overcome, should it be that overcoming the adversities mattered, should overcoming them mean anything to him or to M.E..

For, with his friend's death, Bastard's burden had doubled. And he knew that this was okay. He exhaled deeply. He felt tired but alert.

The elevator produced another DING and halted its descent. And then he remembered, he knew exactly what he had to do next, and this gave him great comfort because he had never known anything with such certainty before.

And with that conviction he discovered a newlyfound sense of peace. It was something that he had never before experienced.

Bastard looked at his friends and smiled as he took off his gloves and waited for the next sounds.

EPILOGUE

Lance Newcomb and Miguel Evangelista died at the courthouse. Bastard threw me the brick as he was gunned down outside. Apparently, Sasia Stasia and NNannette Nonet were able to escape. Dunno what happened to Despi. I'm fine, thank you. So is Curiosity.

ABOUT THE AUTHOR

Stefan O. Rak lives in New York City, because it makes sense.

In the 1940s, his grandparents fled Ukraine for NYC, otherwise he may have never been born. As a child, some neurologists suspected that he had hypergraphia, but it turned out that he had other issues. He graduated high school a criminal musician and later got a Masters in Cinema Studies from NYU's Tisch School of the Arts. He's worked as an archival director, film professor, record producer, experimental music programmer, and bartender.

Stefan self-published his first novel, *New Roses*, which he finished in Salzburg, Austria, and at Monet's house in Giverny. He owns a bar in the city, in the neighborhood. At the time of this writing, he was born in 1982. *Adventures of Bastard and M.E.* is his second novel.

ABOUT THE PUBLISHER

Whisk(e)y Tit is committed to restoring degradation and degeneracy to the literary arts. We work with authors who are unwilling to sacrifice intellectual rigor, unrelenting playfulness, and visual beauty in our literary pursuits, often leading to texts that would otherwise be abandoned in today's largely homogenized literary landscape. In a world governed by idiocy, our commitment to these principles is an act of civil service and civil disobedience alike.